"Maybe We Could Touch More,"

Jesse suggested. "You know, to convince the family."

"We held hands last night," Holly said. "What should we do differently?"

"I want you to flirt with me."

Holly fluttered her eyelashes. "Like this?"

Jesse laughed.

Holly knew how to flirt. She also knew flirting could sometimes be dangerous. "If I flirt, you won't think I'm coming on to you?"

"Of course not. No more than my kissing you means I'm coming on to you."

His words registered about the same time he moved his mouth onto hers.

Dear Reader,

As a very special treat this season, Silhouette Desire is bringing you the best in holiday stories. It's our gift from us—the editorial staff at Silhouette—to you, the readers. The month begins with a very special MAN OF THE MONTH from Ann Major, *A Cowboy Christmas*. Years ago, a boy and girl were both born under the same Christmas star. She grew up rich; he grew up poor…and when they met, they fell into a love that would last a lifetime….

Next, Anne McAllister's CODE OF THE WEST series continues with *Cowboys Don't Stay*, the third book in her series about the Tanner brothers.

Christmas weddings are always a lot of fun, and that's why we're bringing you *Christmas Wedding* by Pamela Macaluso. And if Texas is a place you'd like to spend the holidays—along with a sexy Texas man— don't miss *Texas Pride* by Barbara McCauley. Next, popular Silhouette Romance writer Sandra Steffen makes her Desire debut with *Gift Wrapped Dad*.

Finally, do not miss *Miracles and Mistletoe*, another compelling love story from the talented pen of Cait London.

So, from our "house" to yours…Happy Holidays.

Lucia Macro

Please address questions and book requests to:
Silhouette Reader Service
U.S.: 3010 Walden Ave., P.O. Box 1325, Buffalo, NY 14269
Canadian: P.O. Box 609, Fort Erie, Ont. L2A 5X3

PAMELA MACALUSO
CHRISTMAS WEDDING

SILHOUETTE *Desire*®
Published by Silhouette Books
America's Publisher of Contemporary Romance

SILHOUETTE BOOKS

ISBN 0-373-05970-1

CHRISTMAS WEDDING

Copyright © 1995 by Pamela Macaluso

This edition published by arrangement with Harlequin Books S.A.

® and TM are trademarks of Harlequin Books S.A., used under license. Trademarks indicated with ® are registered in the United States Patent and Trademark Office, the Canadian Trade Marks Office and in other countries.

Printed in U.S.A.

PAMELA MACALUSO

wanted to be a writer from the moment she realized people actually wrote the wonderful stories that were read to her. Since she is extremely curious and has an overactive imagination, writing is the perfect career for her. Curiosity is a necessary part of "research," and flights of fantasy can be called "plotting"—terms she prefers to nosy and woolgathering.

While she loves movies, Pamela would choose a good book over any other form of entertainment. It sometimes takes a search party to get her out of a library or bookstore.

For: Tom and Cleo Barnes,
Dad and Mother,
who were married on Christmas Day

One

———

Was she seeing things? Or did the two-way mirror looking from the tattoo parlor office into the display area need cleaning?

Holly Bryant was used to seeing attractive men. But this guy was a *major* hunk. From his dark brown hair to his dusty black motorcycle boots—and all parts between. Including his enticing backside, which was displayed to absolute advantage in snug, faded denim.

In keeping with the warm October day in Daytona Beach, Florida, the top half of the man was decked out in a black leather vest. As he turned and walked farther into the shop, Holly could see that the vest showed off his broad shoulders, muscular chest and arms. The V neckline exposed a triangle of dark, curling hair.

And there wasn't a tattoo in sight.

He was looking at the sample tattoo drawings and photographs displayed on the walls.

"Well, what are you waiting for? The guy's a customer and Dad's on lunch break," Holly muttered to herself under her breath. She hoped she could wait on the guy without staring...or drooling all over him.

Opening the door into the front of the shop, she put on her best salesperson smile and walked out. "May I help you?"

He turned and looked at her with intense green eyes, but he didn't smile.

Unusual. She was used to men smiling and flirting with her. Especially when she was decked out in the provocative outfits she wore to work in the tattoo parlor.

She'd been designing and making her own clothes long before she'd started taking fashion design classes at a local art school. For "Daytona Bike Week" and "Biketoberfest" she had a special biker-look wardrobe. It was sexy and daring. She thought of it as costuming for her job...playing a part.

Obviously the part of flirting temptress wasn't working on this customer.

Up close Holly thought he looked vaguely familiar but couldn't place him. Of course, during Daytona Bike Week every March and the more recently added Biketoberfest in October, there were large numbers of repeat visitors year after year and also an occasional celebrity.

This guy was handsome enough to be an actor, but nothing clicked. Or maybe he was one of those cover models from the romance novels her friend Ellen read.

"I don't see anything for Yankee riders," he said. His voice was deep and smooth—the kind of voice that made you think about maple syrup.

"Most of these samples went up ten years ago, when my dad moved to this location. Yankee wasn't around at the time, but he has done Yankee tattoos. If you'll step over here, I have a book showing some of them. Plus, he'll do custom designs, drawn to order or copied from something you bring in."

He flipped through the book, glancing a little longer at the designs showcasing Yankee. Some were renderings of the Yankee logo, others declared the names of different models in decorative lettering: Yankee Clipper, Yankee Spirit, Yankee Pride.

"I take it you ride a Yankee," Holly said.

He kept his position, but he glanced up at her. "Yes, I do."

"They're starting to be more popular. I've seen more on the road this Biketoberfest than at any biker event in the past." *Didn't this guy ever smile?* "It must be all the excitement over the Yankee Hunks."

Now he was really frowning. "Or it might be that more people are starting to realize what great bikes Yankees are." He closed the book.

"Did you see anything you liked?"

"Actually, I was looking for a specific tattoo I saw on a guy this afternoon. He said this is where he'd gotten it done."

"Well, maybe if you described it for me."

"It showed a caricature of a biker and he was holding a picket sign that read Yankee Go Home." If there'd been the smallest hint of good nature on his face, it was gone now.

"Was the guy's name Tiny?"

"Yes."

It seemed like a strange choice for someone who rode a Yankee, but Dad's first rule was that the customer was always right. "Tiny's was the first of that design, and it was just done last week so it's not in the book yet. But I can hunt up the original drawing." Holly kept a perfect poker face as she asked, "And where were you thinking about having it placed?"

He had gorgeous muscular arms that could accommodate a tattoo. Plus there was plenty more body currently hidden from view by denim and leather.

"I was thinking about one of two places. Either the trash can or my attorney's desk."

"Excuse me?"

"Either the design goes, or you'll find yourself being sued."

Holly shrugged, hoping that if she looked calm this whole thing would turn out to be a practical joke or one of those hidden video shows. "I'm sorry you don't like the tattoo, but I'm sure there's no copyright on the phrase 'Yankee go home.'"

"Not the phrase, but that particular rendering of the word Yankee is a registered trademark."

"Are you a lawyer or something?"

"Or something."

Holly realized why he looked so familiar. "You're one of them, aren't you? One of the Yankee Hunks."

He folded his arms across his chest with a rippling of muscles that made Holly's breath catch in her throat. "We prefer to be called co-founders or co-owners."

She pointed to the book. "The other tattoos probably fall under the same trademark laws, do you want them removed, also?"

"I have no objection to the others."

"Because they don't knock your bikes?"

"Exactly."

Holly didn't know enough about the laws to argue with him. "I'll talk to my father about it."

"Is he the one who did the tattoo?"

"He did the tattoo, but I drew the design." Tiny had come in on a busy afternoon. While he was waiting, he'd described what he'd wanted. Holly had made some sample sketches to give her father a general idea to work from. As it turned out, her sketch was exactly what Tiny had wanted, so her father had used it.

"You designed the tattoo?"

"Yes. Now, do you want a tattoo, or not?"

"Not."

"Okay. Well, then, if there's anything else I can do for you, ring the bell on the counter." She turned and went back into the office, muttering under her breath about hunks who thought their good looks gave them a license to be grouchy.

Jesse frowned. His partners, Rorke O'Neil and Alex Dalton, and Yankee's corporate attorney, Chad Ralston, were sitting around the table in a hotel suite overlooking the Atlantic Ocean.

After they went over the daily agenda of their public appearances, Jesse told them about Tiny—who hadn't gotten his nickname for any part of him that showed—and his tattoo. Jesse also told them about his trip to the tattoo parlor.

While he wanted to go for blood, the others didn't seem as incensed by the tattoo as he was. Rorke and Alex actually thought it was funny.

Chad said, "Whether we have a chance of winning a lawsuit is not the issue, Jesse. What we have to consider is what the media will do with it. They'll make it look like three big bad guys are picking on one poor artistic waif."

"This waif is about five foot nine, dressed in black leather and built like a centerfold."

Not to mention her long, luscious legs that made a man wonder how it would feel to have them wrapped around him. Or the long, strawberry-blond hair he would love to see spread across a black satin pillowcase. And the full, pouty lips, which under normal circumstances he would have wanted a taste of.

Chad interrupted his thoughts. "It doesn't matter. They'll make her look like Little Red Riding Hood. All sweet, trusting innocence."

"Besides," Rorke said. "If we make a big deal out of this thing, they'll start broadcasting the picture and more people will see it. Once it gets that much exposure other people might decide they want one, too."

"And then it will end up on T-shirts," Alex said.

"Baseball hats," Rorke said.

"Coffee mugs," Alex added.

Jesse looked at Rorke. "Don't you dare say refrigerator magnets."

"I was going to say bumper stickers, but refrigerator magnets are good."

"Chad, be the voice of reason in this wilderness," Jesse said.

"As I told you before, Jesse, I really think the best thing for us to do would be to ignore this particular tattoo," Chad said.

Maybe the sight of Chad and his briefcase would be enough to scare her into throwing out the design. "Could you at least go over there with me and take a look at the drawing?"

Chad shrugged. "I don't see what good it will do, but you're the boss."

Jesse looked at his agenda for the next day. "Tomorrow at two o'clock, then?"

Holly made an appreciative sound as she washed her face free of her at-work makeup. The extra makeup went along with the sexy image of her clothes. She liked the effect, but by the end of her shift she was always ready to get rid of it. After toweling dry, she smoothed on some moisturizer and brushed on light brown mascara.

She changed into a colorful camp shirt and khaki walking shorts and braided her hair. Picking up her backpack, she headed for class.

Holly paused briefly on the front porch of the white-clapboard house. At one time the house had been a large, single-family home, but then had been converted into apartments. Similar changes had been made to most of the houses on the block, including the one next door where her father lived.

It was a nice arrangement having Red in the next building, giving them both the privacy of living alone while allowing them to share a car. They each had their own motorcycle for regular transportation, but they shared the car on those few days when the Florida weather wasn't conducive to motorcycle riding. Holly usually took the car to school because it was easier to transport her portfolio back and forth.

Once in the car, she drove the familiar oak-and palm-lined route to school. She caught herself checking every motorcycle she passed. It was normal for her to look at the bikes, but today she was also looking for a particular biker.

Jesse Tyler. A Yankee Hunk with an attitude.

She'd looked through a stack of motorcycle magazines her father kept at the shop until she'd found one with a picture of the Yankee owners. The man who'd been in the shop today was Jesse Tyler. Two months ago, when the article had been published, he was the only one of the three owners who was still single.

So what?

The guy hadn't looked twice at her. Besides, she wasn't interested in getting involved with any man. She had a career to build and didn't need the hassle of dealing with a member of the opposite sex at this point in her life. From what she'd seen her friends go through, she couldn't imagine any man being worth the trouble and heartache they brought with them.

But Jesse sure was a pleasure to look at. She hoped she didn't have the opportunity to watch him from opposite sides of a courtroom.

With his usual endearing optimism, her father had told her not to worry about lawsuit threats, but Holly couldn't help it.

She wished she had promised Jesse they wouldn't use the design again. She would have, but his attitude had annoyed her. If he'd asked nicely, instead of demanded, she probably would have complied.

And if he'd been the least bit congenial, she might have been able to ask him about the rumor going around school that Yankee Motorworks might be adding a line of motorcycle clothing to their business. It would be an incredible coup if she could get in on the ground floor of such a project.

It would be the chance she wanted—to make a name for herself.

Once she'd found her own success, she could stop worrying that she might fall into the trap of basing her self-worth on the man in her life. Her mother had done it; Holly was determined not to.

And once she established her self-worth, she wouldn't repeat her mother's mistake. She wouldn't have to leave broken relationships, and possibly children, behind to upgrade the man in her life.

She turned into the school parking lot, pushing away all thoughts of her future, her mother, and Jesse Tyler from her mind. Leaving her free to concentrate on the class ahead.

The next afternoon Holly was putting the finishing touches on a pencil sketch of a jacket for her midterm project when the ringing of the bell by the front door signaled that someone had come into the shop.

"Holly, can you get that?" Red Bryant called out to her.

"Sure, Dad."

There were two men wearing business suits in the display area. One stood just inside the door, facing the window. The other, holding a briefcase, stood by the counter. Holly guessed he was in his late thirties or early forties. Medium brown hair, deep brown eyes—he was attractive in an Ivy League sort of way.

He gave her a visual once-over, then glanced over his shoulder at the other man before turning to her again. He smiled.

"May I help you?" she asked.

He pulled a business card from his pocket and laid it on the counter. "Chad Ralston. I represent Yankee Motorworks."

Holly's heart sank to her toes. She picked up the card, trying to look casual.

Stay calm. Don't let him see he's got you rattled.

"So, what can we do for you, Mr. Ralston? A tattoo of a nice heart that says Mother? Or perhaps a shark? How about a great white?" The words poured out before she could stop them.

The man by the window laughed, then turned and walked toward them.

Holly was bowled over again by how good-looking Jesse was—even in today's civilized business attire. But she would sleep on a bed of tattoo needles before she let him know she thought so. "Oh, so you like lawyer jokes, Mr. Tyler?"

When the laughter stopped, his face took its grim lines again. "It appears so, Ms. . . ."

"Bryant. Holly Bryant."

"I brought Chad in to see the design we discussed yesterday."

"You'll have to take him to see Tiny."

"You said you had a copy."

"I *had* the original drawing. I don't anymore." It was at home, hanging on her refrigerator, and the picket sign now read Jesse Tyler Go Home.

Chad shrugged. "I guess that's it, then."

Jesse held up one hand. "Hold on a minute." He turned to Chad. "What's to keep her from drawing it again?"

Holly planted a fist on each hip. "You can't stop me from drawing anything."

"Chad?"

"She's right. She can draw it." He turned to Holly. "But you can't sell it or use it in any way to profit your business."

"And what if I do?" The words were for Chad Ralston, but her eyes were on Jesse.

Holly felt her father's hands settle on her shoulders. "Good afternoon, gentlemen." He stepped to the side and held his hand out across the counter. "Red Bryant." He shook hands with Chad and then Jesse. He was about the same height as the other men, but he had an extra twenty years and an extra fifty pounds on them. "What can we do for you today?"

Jesse answered. "We've asked Ms. Bryant not to reproduce a particular design. If she agrees, then we can all avoid the cost and headache of a lawsuit."

Holly looked at her dad. "Tiny's tattoo... I mentioned it yesterday."

Red nodded. "I remember. Why don't you go on into the stockroom and unpack the shipment and let me handle this?"

She looked at Jesse. The urge was there to spout philosophical ideals about artistic freedom of expression, but at the moment artistic freedom was balanced against her father's livelihood, and she didn't feel it was her place to jeopardize that.

Especially when the probability was that even if the sample drawing were in the shop she doubted there would be many requests for it. Tiny's girlfriend had run off with a guy who rode a Yankee, which was why he'd come up with the idea in the first place.

Holly looked at her dad. "All right, but call if you need me."

Ten minutes later her father joined her in the stockroom.

"Are they gone?"

"Yes."

She set aside the packing list she was holding. "Well? What did they say?"

"For the most part, they repeated what they'd said to you."

"You were listening?"

"I heard the whole conversation."

"And what did you say?"

"I told them I wouldn't use the design again."

All artistic freedom and philosophical issues aside, it was the most logical solution. "Were they satisfied with that?"

"The lawyer seemed to be, but Mr. Tyler said he'd be happier if he'd heard it from you personally."

"I'm sorry, Dad. I should have said it, but something about the guy annoyed me."

"I noticed. You were uncharacteristically edgy."

"Edgy? I'm never edgy."

"I know. That's why it was such a surprise." He placed his hand on her shoulder. "Hopefully we've seen the last of them."

Holly hoped so, too.

Or did she?

Two

Jesse was glad when Biketoberfest ended and he could get back to his real work—designing and planning the next generation of Yankees. Sales were rising, and their racing team was holding its own. But, the way he saw it, there was always room for improvement.

He had been spending long hours at work. It kept him from having to think about the shambles his once-active social life was in.

That blasted Yankee Hunk thing!

Jesse, Rorke and Alex had posed in full-faced helmets for a Yankee ad campaign. No one had expected the furor that had followed as all around the country women asked, "Who are those guys?" Once their identities were known, all hell had broken loose.

He'd always had a way with the ladies. But after the ad campaign there were more willing women than ever pursuing him. Unfortunately, rather than wanting *him*, the women were after the mystique of the Yankee Hunk. And just as he hadn't wanted the Tyler family fortune handed to him on a silver platter, he wasn't interested in women lusting after his image. Women who claimed undying love when they didn't even know him.

He couldn't even share the frustration with Rorke and Alex. With the phenomenal growth of the business, they all lived in different states now. Besides, Rorke had gotten married before the trouble had started, and Alex had tied the knot shortly after the news had broken.

Oh, well, he liked getting more work done, but other than that, his self-imposed celibacy was no picnic.

On this Saturday morning in November as he read the newspaper and thought about whether to go on a motorcycle ride or put in a few more hours at work, the phone rang. He considered letting the answering machine get it, but ended up picking up the receiver.

"Hello?"

"Hi, Jesse. It's Joanna."

Jesse smiled. The rest of his family had turned their backs on him when he'd gone into the motorcycle business, but he and his younger sister had stayed in touch and kept a close relationship in spirit if not in distance. "Hi, sweetheart. What can I do for you?"

"I have a really big favor to ask. Please don't say no."

"I'll try not to. You know that."

"Douglas proposed. We're getting married in December, and I want you to be in the wedding party."

Joanna and Douglas had visited him one weekend. He'd liked the other man well enough and could tell the two of them were crazy about each other. "Are you eloping to Vegas or Reno?" While he meant it as a joke, he couldn't help thinking it would make his life so much easier if it were true.

"No, we're getting married in Florida. At Dad and Mom's."

"JoJo—"

"Don't say no, Jesse. I asked Dad and Mom. They said all right."

"Can I have that in writing?"

"Jesse!"

He closed his eyes and shook his head. His parents' house was the last place on earth he wanted to go. Actually, it ran a close second to the center of an active volcano. "Sweetheart, you know I wish you and Doug all the best—"

"I want you there...please?"

How could he say no? "All right."

"You'll come?"

"Yes. I'll come."

"Doug, he said he'd come!" Joanna called out. "Doug says he's glad. Now, I want you to come down the week before, so we can do the tuxedo measurement thing and you can help me with all the last-minute stuff."

"Isn't that what bridesmaids are for?"

"Oh, they'll be here, too. But you're my brother. I want you around the last week."

"I can have my measurements taken here and faxed to you, then come down the morning of the wedding. How's that?"

"Jesse—"

"Don't you dare say please again, Joanna. I'll think about it and let you know."

"Okay. Oh, and bring a date if you want."

Later that same afternoon Jesse was thinking about his conversation with his sister and wishing the whole wedding was over and done with. He knew the family event would attract Tylers from all around the country.

He pictured them all outside soaking up the December Florida sunshine. Suddenly the growl of a motorcycle engine catches their attention. He rides up the driveway on his red Yankee.

Sitting on the passenger seat behind him would be his "date." Her body pressed against him, her hair flowing out behind.

Of course it couldn't really happen this way. Not with helmet laws, but this was his fantasy so her hair could flutter in the breeze.

He sat up with a jolt when he realized the woman's hair was strawberry blond....

Holly turned her Harley-Davidson into the parking lot of the tattoo shop. Parking to the far right, she left the center spaces for customers. There was a Jeep Cherokee in one of them, and her father's bike was on the far left.

She set the bike on its kickstand and got off. Reaching into one of the leather saddlebags, she pulled out the bag of fabric samples she'd collected for use in a homework assignment. If it was a slow afternoon at work, she would be able to get started on it. One of the perks of working in a family business.

After entering the shop, it took her eyes a moment to adjust to the dimmer lighting. When they did, she saw her father standing next to Jesse Tyler.

Was he here about the lawsuit again?

Jesse was wearing a business suit, which made her nervous.

But her father was smiling. That was a good sign.

She walked past the men and went to stand behind the counter, tucking her bag onto one of the shelves. "Change your mind about a tattoo, Mr. Tyler?"

"No, I was hoping to take you out for coffee. There's a business proposition I'd like to discuss with you."

Were the rumors true that Yankee was looking into creating a line of clothing? Had he found out she was studying to be a designer?

Holly slammed on her mental brakes before her imagination could get carried away any further with the unlikely scenario.

But whatever did he mean by "a business proposition"? "Can we talk here? I've just come back from my lunch break."

Red spoke up. "Things have been slow. Go ahead and take an extended lunch."

"But—"

"I insist."

Holly shrugged. "All right, then."

They walked to the door. Jesse held it open for her.

"Where to?" she asked.

"How's the Coffee Bean?"

The Coffee Bean was a trendy spot specializing in a variety of flavored coffees, espresso, cappuccino and desserts. It was about a mile from the shop. "That's fine."

Jesse looked toward where Holly had parked. "Is that your bike?"

"Yes." She was proud of her purple and silver Harley-Davidson FXR Low Rider.

"That's a lot of motorcycle for a woman."

"I'm aware of that, but I can handle it."

She thought he was going to say more. Instead he helped her into the front seat of the Cherokee, then went around and got into the driver's seat.

Holly watched him as he drove, his movements controlled and precise. She wondered if he rode his motorcycle that way, too...or if he made love that way.

When the silence got to be too much, she asked, "What is it you wanted to discuss? Tiny's tattoo?"

Jesse kept his eyes on the road. "I'm afraid I can't discuss the tattoo or any pending lawsuit without my lawyer present. What I want to talk about is a job offer of sorts."

She was tempted to point out that she had a job working for her father, but the slim chance that it might be a fashion design job he was talking about kept her quiet.

Their arrival at their destination cut the conversation short, and the subject didn't come up again until they had been seated and had given their orders to the waitress.

"Now then, Ms. Bryant, how would you like a one-week, all-expenses-paid trip to Lake Wyndham? Plus salary."

The mention of the exclusive south Florida community, second only to Palm Beach in its wealth and old money status, made Holly suspicious. "Just what would this job entail?"

"Essentially, it's an acting job."

"An acting job. Shouldn't you call a talent agent?"

"Let's say I'm typecasting."

"Typecasting? Why would you be looking for someone to play a tattoo artist's assistant?"

"I'm looking for a woman to play the part of my fiancée for a week."

She tilted her head to one side. "You think I look like the kind of woman you would marry?" The article she'd glanced at to learn his identity had linked his name with a prominent performance artist, several supermodels and a politician's daughter.

He paused. "You look like the type of woman my parents would expect me to marry."

She wanted to ask what kind of parents he had.

Jesse had only seen her in her black leather biker outfits and the hot pink jumpsuit she was wearing today—her work costumes. Would she be dressing this way in Lake Wyndham?

Would her school wardrobe be appropriate, or would she have to dig out some of the clothes she wore on visits to her mother and stepfather? But he said he was typecasting... "If I look the part, I'm assuming I don't need a new wardrobe for the trip?"

"Everything I've seen you in would be fine. If you'd like, though, I'll throw in a clothing allowance on top of the salary. All I ask is that you don't pick anything stuffy or conservative."

Now she was really curious about his parents. She knew anything he'd seen her in would shock most of the Lake Wyndham crowd. "I don't know. Can I think about this and get back to you?"

He took out a business card. "I'll put the dates here on the back." He held the card out to her.

She took it. The tips of her fingers brushed briefly against his. His skin was warm. She wondered what it would feel like to hold hands with him.

If they were pretending to be engaged, wouldn't there be at least that much, and probably more, physical contact between them? She tucked the card into her pocket. "Just how far does this acting job go? I mean, you're not expecting me to sleep with you or anything?"

A streak of color highlighted each cheekbone. "Ms. Bryant, I'm offering a legitimate business deal. What you're suggesting would be illegal."

And I'll bet the implication that you might be trying to pay me to have sex with you really ties your boxers in a knot, too. Besides, if he'd just lighten up and smile once in a while he could probably charm his way into any bed he wanted. She was sure he had a killer smile.

The waitress arrived with their coffee. Holly thought she fussed too much over Jesse, making sure his cup was lined up just so. It was the sort of thing a fiancée would notice.

Maybe she could pull it off, even without formal acting experience.

Once the woman left, Jesse continued. "You'll have your own bedroom and the place has so many servants, you'll think you're in a hotel. We'll need to spend some time together. Engaged couples do that sort of thing, I believe. But I'll be sure you have time off to pursue your own recreational interests. There are horses, a sailboat, and the beach is about an hour away."

Holly sipped her coffee. "You make it sound very tempting."

"Good."

"Earlier you mentioned a salary?"

He named a figure much higher than what she normally made in a week. With tuition for the next term coming up, she could use the money. And the shop could use some remodeling.

Such a large sum for only a week's work...if you could call a week of playing "Lifestyles of the Rich and Famous" work.

The life-style was not completely unknown to Holly. When she was eight, her mother had left her tattoo-artist father and married a successful Florida land developer. Holly had visited them and their four children several times a year. While there, she'd acted and dressed the part of dutiful stepdaughter.

Other than that, she had little to do with them. Although she was certain they would give her money for school and probably for the remodeling, too, if she asked. After high school they'd offered her money to continue her education instead of delaying until she'd saved enough on her own.

Then, as now, she knew her father would have a fit if she took their money. He might frequently be short of the green stuff, but he was long on pride.

"You do make it tempting. But I need to think about this."

She looked like the kind of woman his parents would expect him to marry.

What exactly had he meant by that?

Holly's best friend Ellen worked at the library. The two had been close since elementary school. Holly knew she could trust Ellen not to tell anyone about Jesse's offer. So she called her and asked her to find information about Jesse, especially anything on his family.

Ellen had a whole stack of things for her when Holly stopped by the library after work. Two hours later, after reading through a number of magazine and newspaper articles, she had the story.

Ultrarich family. Millions made on railroads way back when by enterprising ancestors, now maintained by investments. The family was currently into breeding and training polo ponies.

Instead of blending into the family business and life-style, their eldest child, Jesse, became a motorcycle enthusiast in high school, then went on to study engineering in college. With Rorke O'Neil, he built a prototype motorcycle. They added a third partner, Alex Dalton, and founded Yankee Motorworks.

The family had had a fit. It was bad enough Jesse was working for a living, but to have the Tyler name associated with motorcycles was more than they could stand. It made no difference to them that many rich and famous people were now cruising the roads on two wheels—it was not appropriate for *their* son. When Jesse persisted, they cut off his trust funds and wrote him out of their wills. Since then they'd had little or no contact with him.

With her usual softhearted tendency to side with the underdog, Holly was immediately sympathetic to Jesse. She was willing to overlook the fact that the man was probably getting ready to sue her and that he was handsomer than any man had the right to be.

All she saw was his rich, powerful parents trying to control him and make him live their choices for his life and not his own.

"This is interesting," Ellen said.

Holly looked at the newspaper Ellen was holding. It was an engagement announcement. Joanna Tyler and Douglas Wellington. The wedding was to be in December at the home of the bride's parents in Lake Wyndham, Florida.

A smile tugged at the edges of her mouth. She didn't like Jesse much, but although he'd missed the humor in Tiny's tattoo, the guy did have a sense of humor about some things.

Ellen reached her arms above her head and stretched. "When did you say he wanted you to go with him?"

"The week before, through the day after this wedding."

"What are you going to do?"

"I probably need my head examined, but I'm seriously thinking about going."

Ellen held up a magazine with a picture of the three Yankee owners on the front. "There are worse guys to be stuck pretending to be in love with."

They would be expected to act like they were in love. Holly hadn't thought about that part of it. While she had considered there would be handholding, she hadn't looked at the bigger picture.

Of course if she gazed into his gorgeous green eyes long enough, it would be easy to convince even herself that she was in love with him.

Ellen continued. "Is he as good-looking in person?"

"Better."

"Impossible. Do you think you'll get a chance to meet his partners?"

"He didn't say. But you can stop drooling, the other two are already married."

"So, are you going to do it?"

"I don't know. What do you think?"

"I think you should. Besides getting paid, you'll probably have fun. And maybe if you get on his good side, you can convince him not to file charges."

She might also be able to get information on the rumored Yankee clothing line. If she were spending time with Jesse, maybe she could get the inside scoop and possibly a foot in the door for a job.

"Oh, I guess I'll go."

"You make it sound like a sacrifice. Most women would be willing to pay *him* for the chance you're getting."

Holly knew Ellen was right. Yet she couldn't quite shake all her misgivings. She looked at one of the magazines on the table, opened to an article titled Billionaire's Renegade Son Makes His First Million.

There was more to Jesse Tyler than met the eye, that was for sure. What would it be like to spend a week with him?

"Mr. Tyler, Mr. Dalton is on line one."

"Thanks." Jesse picked up the phone. "What can I do for you, Alex?"

They discussed Alex's idea to offer public tours of the Daytona Beach facilities. The issue would be brought up at their next board meeting, but since Jesse was most familiar with the setup down there, Alex had called to verify some details.

"How's Genie?" Jesse asked after the business was taken care of.

"Fine. We've got our first anniversary coming up in December."

"That's right. Congratulations." Man, the last year had flown by. "Speaking of December, I'm planning to take a week off for my sister's wedding."

"You're going to your sister's wedding?" Both of his partners knew about his estrangement from his family.

"Joanna asked me to be in the wedding party."

"Be sure to have a good time."

"Hey, you know me. I *always* have a good time."

Alex was quiet for a moment. "You *used to* always have a good time."

"So, how's Rorke doing?" Jesse changed the subject.

"Callie is due sometime in December. I was there last week, and Rorke already has a model train set up."

It would be a while before Rorke and Callie's son or daughter was ready for a model train, but there was something heartening about parents who were so excited about the arrival of their children that they went overboard—as opposed to parents who ignored their kids most of the time, then went overboard to ease their consciences.

But he didn't want to think about his parents now. He would be seeing them soon. After finishing his conversation with Alex, he looked at the calendar, counting the days before he left for Lake Wyndham.

He hadn't heard from Holly yet.

Jesse was surprised she hadn't jumped at his offer. Surprised, but pleased. The way she wanted to consider her decision meant she was looking at it as a business deal and not as some women would—as a way to try to bring him to heel.

Of course, he hadn't expected that from Holly. He'd felt a negative tension from her the times they'd been together. He assumed it was the possible lawsuit that kept her from liking him.

But whatever the reason, it was best that she didn't. He needed a pretend fiancée for a week. He didn't need another woman falling in love with him.

Three

Holly stared at her phone. She'd decided to accept Jesse's offer, but inexplicably hesitated over notifying him.

She snatched the receiver and pushed the buttons before she could chicken out. A secretary answered Jesse's phone, but rather than having to leave a message, Holly was put right through.

"Ms. Bryant, what can I do for you?"

Over the phone his deep voice had an added warmth she hadn't noticed in person. "If we're going to be engaged, shouldn't we be on a first-name basis?"

"Holly, then. You're accepting the offer?" Jesse said. He sounded pleased.

"Yes."

"Good. Are you free Saturday morning?"

Holly glanced at the calendar hanging next to the phone. "This Saturday?"

"Yes. We need to buy an engagement ring and go over the information engaged couples would know about each other. It should only take a few hours."

A fiancée would most likely know what that heavenly body looked like without clothes and what kind of a lover Jesse was.

She cleared her throat before answering. "I have to be at work by one o'clock."

"I'll pick you up at nine-thirty. If you'll give me your address and directions."

"Why don't I meet you at Dad's shop? That way, if we run behind schedule, I won't be late to work."

"Whatever you prefer."

"Nine-thirty at the shop, then."

"See you there."

Saturday morning Holly changed clothes three times before settling on a colorful tourist look. Jesse couldn't complain that it was conservative. At the same time a salesclerk in the jewelry store was more likely to take her seriously than if she were in her biker clothes.

She couldn't remember how old she'd been the first time she'd realized that much of the world looked at the way you were dressed and judged you from that. It didn't seem fair, but rather than complain about something she couldn't change, she simply used it to her advantage when she could, and played games and experimented with it the rest of the time.

When she arrived at the tattoo shop, Jesse was already there. He was also dressed somewhere between "decked out" and blue jeans. She could tell from the fit and the fabric that his clothes were top of the line.

They exchanged greetings, then set off.

"Would you like to start with a brief family history, or shall I go first?" Jesse asked.

"I don't have much to tell. I was born and raised in Daytona Beach. You've met my dad. He and my mother were divorced when I was eight. She remarried and has a new family."

"Did the court give custody of you to your father, or did you have a choice?"

"I got to choose."

"I would have guessed an eight-year-old girl would be more likely to pick her mother."

"I've always gotten along much better with my father." That was only part of the reason she'd chosen to stay with him after the divorce. The rest was that, with her eight-year-old logic, she hadn't thought it fair that after the divorce her mother would have Howard and her father wouldn't have anyone.

She hadn't realized at the time that being the single father of a daughter might not be the easiest of circumstances for Red Bryant. All she'd known was that she hadn't wanted to leave him alone.

"Your father never remarried?"

"No, he dates occasionally, but never anything serious. He's really into his work." Holly suspected her father was still carrying a torch for her mother.

"Do you see your mother?" Jesse asked.

"Several times a year I spend a few days with them. Mostly because she feels obligated to invite me. And I go because I feel obligated to accept."

"Have you been working for your father long?"

"I've always been around the shop doing odds and ends, but I didn't actually start on a regular basis until I was in high school. Dad needed someone to work the counter, and I needed to start saving money to put myself through school. Since we get along so well anyway, it seemed like a good solution."

He glanced at her. "You're a student?"

"Part-time, at night."

"Let's leave that bit of information out when you meet my family."

"You don't want them to know I go to school?"

"It sounds too respectable."

Holly fought back a smile. He was bound and determined to present his parents with a fiancée worthy of a renegade son. "Maybe you should tell me a little about my soon-to-be, make-believe prospective in-laws."

He didn't mention that he'd been disinherited, but he did tell her how his career choice had estranged him from his family—except his younger sister Joanna. Holly was surprised he didn't sound bitter. Of course, the fact that he'd gone on to find success on his own might have something to do with it.

"Besides my parents and sister, there will more than likely be a whole collection of aunts, uncles and cousins. Since I don't see them anymore, it won't be expected that you would know much about them. I can fill you in as we go along."

He pulled into the mall parking lot. Since it was early, they found a spot close to the entrance. Once inside, they walked side by side, past a variety of stores decorated for Christmas, until they reached the jewelry store.

As Jesse was about to step into the store, Holly reached out her hand to stop him. The heat radiating from him stunned her and she pulled back quickly.

One dark brow quirked and a knowing smile came onto his face. "You're going to have to work on that."

"On what?"

"Being able to touch me without jumping as though you expect me to attack you." He reached one hand toward her shoulder.

She moved away. "Fine. We'll work on it, but not here." She glanced around to be sure no one was watching. Leaning toward him, she spoke quietly, "Do we need to use aliases in there?"

"Aliases?" He laughed.

The sound surprised Holly, but she liked it. Liked it a lot.

And even though she took her question seriously, she had to smile. "In case someone recognizes you."

He shrugged. "If it happens, it happens. We'll just play it by ear." He nodded toward the store. "Ready?"

Half an hour later Holly and Jesse had looked at so many engagement rings, she suspected that if the salesclerk started bringing the same rings back, they wouldn't even realize it.

The salesclerk smiled, but Holly was sure he was as tired as she was. "I have one more tray, sir. If you'll wait just one moment."

Once the man was out of earshot, Holly asked, "Just what is it you're looking for?"

"Something expensive and gaudy."

The description fit most of the rings they'd seen. "Don't make it too awful. We're going to have to look at it for a week."

The salesclerk returned. A ring in the upper left-hand corner caught Holly's eye. It had a substantial-sized diamond, with a sprinkling of smaller diamonds, emeralds and rubies on either side. When it caught the light, it looked like a snowflake sitting on a bed of holly.

Holly picked it up and slipped it on. It fit perfectly. She held it out for Jesse to see. "It looks like holly."

The clerk perked up. "A lovely ring, miss. And so appropriate with your name being Holly and your getting engaged so close to Christmas."

But Jesse didn't seem impressed. He looked at the tray. Reaching out, he picked up another ring. "Try this one."

Holly reluctantly took off the ring she was wearing and returned it to its spot. She took the one Jesse held. It also slid smoothly into place as if it belonged there. Although it sparkled and shone, she didn't feel connected to it the way she had the holly ring.

Holly ring? Get a grip, Holly, dear. This is a pretend engagement ring for a pretend engagement....

She held her hand toward Jesse. "What do you think? Do you like this one?"

"It works for me. How about you?"

It was too ostentatious for her taste, but she could live with it for a week. "If you're happy, I am."

"All right." Jesse turned to the clerk. "We'll take this one."

"Will that be cash or charge, sir?"

Jesse pulled out his wallet and handed the clerk a credit card. "Charge."

The clerk locked the ring tray into the glass display case, then headed for the cash register.

Holly leaned forward and took another look at the holly ring.

"I'll buy it for you if you'd like. You can tuck it away in your hope chest until you meet the man you're really going to marry."

Holly straightened, turning her back on the case. She'd watched her friends go through painful relationships and wasn't interested...thank you very much. Maybe once she had her career on track, she would look for an equally established and settled man. Someone kind and considerate....

Her gaze drifted to the display window where a ceramic Santa stood—his burlap sack stuffed to overflowing with glittering jewelry.

Kind, considerate, established and settled—yes, that's what she wanted in a man.

"No, thanks." She looked at Jesse. "That's a generous offer, but since the only guy I'd even consider marrying would be Santa Claus, save your money."

Jesse laughed, again. That was twice in one day. Holly wondered if they were setting any records. Sarcasm aside, she felt a thrill of power knowing she'd been the one to make him laugh...and smile.

He was still smiling at her. And she'd been right, he had a killer smile.

A lady-killer smile!

Once the required ring shopping was out of the way, they strolled slowly through the mall. Christmas carols played over the loudspeakers, and the smell of pine-scented potpourri beckoned to them from every shop they passed.

With all the seasonal enticements, it was hard for Holly not to slip into the Christmas shopping mode. But she deliberately focused herself on the task at hand—for the two of them to share more information about themselves with each other.

"Do you live with your father?" Jesse asked.

"I have my own apartment, but we live on the same street. I'll bet you have a big oceanfront house with floor-to-ceiling picture windows across the back." It was where she would live if she had the money for it—plus enough for hurricane insurance.

"No, I have a town house near the Yankee plant on the west side of Daytona Beach. Another in Tucson and an apartment in New York City."

"Why Tucson and New York?"

"We have another plant in Tucson and our headquarters is in New York. I split my time over the three places."

"Do you like all the traveling?"

"I don't mind it."

"That doesn't mean you like it."

He chuckled. "Quite the stickler for details, aren't you, Ms. Bryant?"

She held her left hand up, wiggling her fingers. The diamonds on the "engagement" ring sparkled. "Holly," she reminded him.

"As I said. A stickler for details." He took hold of her hand, weaving their fingers together.

Holly's first instinct was to pull away, but as he'd pointed out earlier, she needed to get over her reticence to touching him. They were supposedly engaged to be married, people would expect them to touch—would think it odd if they didn't. Besides, it wasn't like she'd never held hands with a guy before.

She had . . . but it had never felt like this!

Jesse's hand was large and warm around hers. She was surprised by how much larger, since he was only four inches taller than her own five-nine.

"Now, where were we?" Jesse asked.

In paradise. The words popped so quickly into her mind, Holly was afraid for a moment that she would say them out loud. "I—I asked whether you liked all the traveling you did for work."

He was quiet before answering. "At the moment, yes, I do. But sooner or later I think I'll settle down in one spot."

"When you get married and start a family?"

His brows pulled together and his eyes narrowed.

Holly had the feeling she'd wandered into territory he considered off limits and decided to change the subject. "So, where did you grow up? Lake Wyndham?"

"We came to Florida off and on during the winter months. The rest of the year, home was in Kentucky."

"What about your favorite colors, books, movies, music, ice-cream flavors, pizza toppings?"

"My family wouldn't know the answers to those questions. So, if the subjects should arise, make something up. They'll never know the difference."

"Make something up?"

"That or twist the conversation around and get them talking about themselves."

"I get the feeling you don't like your family very much."

His grip on her hand tightened, as did the muscles along his jawline. Holly didn't think he was aware of either.

"It's none of your business how I feel about my family. You're being paid to convince them you're the love of my life and that's it."

He certainly didn't look like a man in love, but Holly didn't think he would appreciate her pointing it out. "I thought it might help if I knew a little more about the situation."

"You know as much as you need to."

"All right. But this information sharing *was* your idea. Now, if we're done, why don't you take me back to the shop?"

Jesse shrugged. They made the trip to the parking lot in silence. As they neared the Jeep, he let go of her hand to dig into his pocket for the keys.

It had begun to feel so natural, she'd forgotten they'd been holding hands.

On the drive back to the shop, Jesse said, "I hope the weather holds for our ride down. If it doesn't, we'll have to trailer the bike. I'll let you know the day before.''

"We're going to be riding down to Lake Wyndham on your motorcycle?''

"Yes, it's only about a five-hour ride. Since you're used to being on a bike, I didn't think it would be a problem.''

"It's not. Except how are we going to carry a week's worth of clothes for each of us?''

"I'll send the suitcases by courier the day before.''

"Now why didn't I think of that?''

"You don't make many long-distance trips on your bike, do you?''

"Dad and I rode up to Sturgis, South Dakota, one year for a motorcycle meet. I wore one set of clothes, carried a second set in my saddlebag and washed them every night.''

"I went to Sturgis one year.''

"On your Yankee?''

"It was before Yankee existed.'' He glanced at her. "I used to ride a Harley-Davidson Fatboy.''

Well, there was a tidbit of biographical information. She guessed she was going to have to collect it piece by piece.

Holly looked at the glittering ring on her left hand. *I hope you know what you're doing, kiddo.*

Jesse rolled over and looked at the clock. The alarm would be making its annoying noise in three minutes. He reached out and clicked it off before it had a chance to screech at him.

Too bad it's not as easy to short-circuit the rest of life's nuisances.

Like family...

He got out of bed and headed for the bathroom. The notion to leave his morning stubble crossed his mind, but he ended up shaving. Showing up with a fiancée was provocation enough, considering who she was.

Holly was a beautiful woman, no doubt about it. But not at all the proper wife for a Tyler. And exactly the type a black-sheep Tyler would hitch himself to.

He could imagine dear Mimi and Jesse Senior when they met their prospective daughter-in-law. He wondered how much hard cash the old man would offer to part with to bribe Holly to break the engagement. He made a mental note to warn her of the possibility.

He didn't want to tell her too much about his family relationships. The other day she'd seemed interested—he hoped she didn't take it upon herself to try to mend any fences. He was perfectly happy not having to put up with them and their disapproval anymore. He'd lived with it for enough years.

The only reason he was going there was for Joanna, and Joanna only. He would be civil to the rest of them, but no more than that.

In fact, he would probably spend most of his time with Holly. What the hell, there were worse ways to spend a week. And it might prove interesting.

From what time they'd spent together, he knew Holly was an alluring woman. She sure didn't mince her words. She was up-front and straightforward— the way she'd bit into Chad with the shark jokes, the way she'd said the only man she would marry would be Santa Claus....

But for all her bravado, she had a sweet innocence. Like when she'd wanted to know if they should use aliases.

All that and a body that didn't quit.

His self-imposed celibacy was getting tougher for him. Maybe if Holly offered some extracurricular entertainment he would take her up on it.

Yes, it could turn out to be a very interesting week.

Since the nights and early-morning hours were on the cool side, Holly dressed in black leather pants and knee-high black leather boots decorated with silver chains and conchos. She wore a rust-colored stretch lace bodysuit with a black leather tunic-style jacket that zipped up to her neck, but when unzipped draped open to give a generous view of the bodysuit.

She couldn't believe how quickly time had passed since she and Jesse had shopped for the ring. She'd shown it to Ellen and her father. Ellen was so excited you'd think she was the one going to Lake

Wyndham. Her father had reservations about the whole thing, but after giving his opinion, he'd stepped back and left Holly to make her own choice.

Jesse arrived at her apartment door right on time. He was wearing blue jeans and a brown leather bomber jacket. "Ready to go?"

"I just need to grab my helmet."

"Don't bother. I've brought two."

"All right."

Holly locked her apartment and followed him to his bike. It was a big, mean-looking red motorcycle with chrome and brass detailing.

"Nice."

"Thanks. Ever ridden on a Yankee?"

"Not yet."

Once they were both in their helmets and gloves, Jesse got on the bike. He fired up the engine then held out his hand to help her on.

She took his hand and climbed on behind him.

The bike had an elevated passenger seat—a high/low, or king/queen combination. The passenger got a better view, but on the downside she had her legs at his waist level rather than straddled alongside his legs. Not the most comfortable position when she barely knew the guy.

The vision of Jesse the way he'd looked that first afternoon in the sleeveless black vest came into her mind. She quickly banished it. Settling against the padded sissy bar, she hooked her boots over the buddy pegs and rested her hands on the smooth leather covering her thighs.

He glanced over his shoulder. "Aren't you going to hold on to me?"

Holly quirked one brow. "That old put-your-arms-around-me-and-hold-tight routine only works when there's no sissy bar or a less experienced rider."

He shrugged. "You can't fault a guy for trying."

"Just put it in gear and let's go."

Holly thought she saw the corners of his mouth start to tilt in a smile before he turned to face forward. She settled in for the long ride ahead.

She tried to ignore the friction of her inner legs against Jesse. She'd been on the back of plenty of motorcycles and had never felt anything like this before...this awareness of the man in front of her. An awareness bordering on sexual.

Heck, there was nothing "bordering" about it. It *was* sexual.

She was totally aware of Jesse as a male. Not just another human being, but a male, a member of the opposite sex. Too bizarre.

Deliberately turning her attention to the bike itself, she realized what a smooth ride she was getting. The dips and imperfections in the road were barely noticeable. Of course, that only served to make Jesse's movements more so.

By the time they stopped for gas, Holly wanted nothing more than to fall into his arms.

"Are you ready for lunch?" Jesse asked.

Maybe something as familiar as a burger and fries would help get rid of the totally unfamiliar feelings she was having. "Yes."

"While I finish up here, why don't you go get us a table?"

The coffee shop was right next to the gas station. Holly went on ahead, glad not to be subjecting herself to sitting behind Jesse—after lunch would be soon enough for that.

Suddenly a week seemed like a long time....

Four

———

"Have you always had this effect on women?" Holly asked Jesse as he slid into the booth.

He glanced over his shoulder.

She noticed many of the women quickly shifted their gazes, but some boldly, almost brazenly, continued to look at him.

Jesse shrugged and turned to face her. "It's been worse since the publicity about the billboard."

"You don't seem very happy about it. Most guys would eat it up."

He picked up the menus from the end of the table, handed one to Holly and opened the other. "I'm not most guys."

Boy, that was an understatement. Holly glanced through the menu. While they waited for the waitress to take their order and throughout lunch, she tried without success to get a conversation going.

Jesse answered her questions and asked a few of his own, but she could sense that his mind was a million miles away. She wondered if he was thinking about seeing his parents again. Even though he was an independent, successful man, Holly suspected he might still carry their rejection around as excess emotional baggage.

The only time she was one hundred percent sure she had his undivided attention was when she pulled down the zipper of her jacket. After the way he seemed to ignore the fact she was a woman, it was a real ego soother.

When their waitress delivered the check along with a final flirtatious smile for Jesse, Holly rolled her eyes. "Another conquest."

"It makes me wonder why you're so immune to my apparent charms."

She didn't want to remind him about the threatened lawsuit, and definitely didn't want him suspecting she wasn't as immune as he thought, or as she'd thought, so she dramatically placed her left hand over her heart. "Why, Jesse, dear, I'm wearing your ring. Isn't that proof of my everlasting love and devotion?"

Jesse shook his head, chuckling. "Are you ready to go?"

Would she ever be ready to climb back on that bike with him? "Ready if you are."

The shadow of a smile played along the edges of his mouth. "Let's go, then."

Holly had expected Jesse's parents' home to be large, but she hadn't envisioned anything near the spacious grandeur awaiting her. She'd also imagined meeting his family shortly after their arrival. Instead they were led to their rooms in the guest wing and told cocktails would be at six-thirty, dinner at seven.

Holly stood in the open doorway of the War Admiral Room, looking across the hallway to where Jesse stood in the doorway of the Omaha Room.

"The War Admiral Room?"

"You'd prefer east wing, second floor, second door on the left?"

"I understand why you'd want to name the rooms. But why War Admiral and Omaha?"

"The rooms in this wing are named for horses who have won the Triple Crown. If you're interested, my mother hired someone to write a history of the house. There's probably a copy in your nightstand. If not, let me know and I'll hunt one up for you."

"I'd like to see it, but at the moment what I'd really like is a shower." *A cold one to drown the tingling awareness of him.*

"I think we should talk a few minutes . . . in private?" He gestured toward his room.

Holly entered and gave a slow whistle as she looked around the Omaha Room. "Nice." She walked to the sitting area in front of the fireplace and sat in one of the wing-back chairs.

Jesse sat on a couch covered in matching fabric. "I don't want you to be surprised if my father tries to lure you aside sometime this week and offers you money to break our engagement."

Holly was unable to speak for a moment. "You think your father will try to bribe me?"

"He might." He folded his hands together between his knees and leaned toward her. "And I'll double whatever he offers, if you turn him down flat."

An outraged sputter was all she managed before he continued. "And if you accept his offer, you'll have to use some of that money to get yourself home, and you'll forfeit the salary I've offered, too."

Holly found her voice. "You're really something...." Standing, she began to pace. "I can't believe you think I would do something so underhanded!"

"How should I know what you would do? I hardly know you."

"So you automatically distrust everyone you don't know?"

"For the most part."

"What about innocent until proven guilty?"

"What about watching your back?"

She would have continued to argue, but then it occurred to her that after the way his parents had treated him, it was probably natural for him to be overly suspicious of other people.

Forcing back her anger, she said, "All right, you watch your back, but I promise I'll keep *my* end of our deal."

Jesse frowned. "You're conceding easily. I wouldn't have guessed you were one to back down from an argument."

"Believe me, I'm not. It's just that I can see your side of things here. Parents are such an essential part of our young lives and with the trouble you had with yours and all—"

"Oh, please...spare me the amateur talk-show psychoanalysis." He wasn't shouting, but his voice had increased in volume.

Holly planted a fist on each hip. "Excuse me for trying to be understanding."

Jesse stood and walked toward her. He was several feet away when the door flew open.

An attractive brunette in formal riding gear ran into the room and straight into Jesse's arms.

"Don't you believe in knocking?" The laughter in his voice countered the reproach of his words.

"I didn't want to waste any time. I can't believe you're finally here."

"Neither can I."

They continued to hug. Holly assumed the woman was Jesse's sister. She wondered whether she should quietly slip away, or clear her throat to remind him that she was there.

Jesse took the matter out of her hands when he said, "JoJo, there's someone I want you to meet."

The woman turned, but kept one arm around Jesse.

"Holly, this is my sister, Joanna. Joanna, my fiancée, Holly Bryant."

Joanna's eyes widened. "Fiancée? I didn't know you were engaged. When? How?"

"A while ago and probably the same way you did. I asked and she said yes."

Joanna moved away from Jesse. She hugged Holly and welcomed her to the family. "I'm surprised this hasn't hit the tabloids."

"We haven't made an official announcement. We're trying to avoid the media circus as long as possible."

Joanna nodded. "The last Yankee Hunk tying the knot is going to create a stir."

"That's why we're keeping a low profile."

"When's the wedding? I hope I'm going to be invited. Maybe we could have a double wedding. There's almost a week left—"

"Whoa, slow down. No double wedding. You'll be invited, but Holly wants a small wedding up in Daytona Beach."

Holly hadn't given the matter much thought, but now she thought about it, she would prefer a small, intimate wedding. "Yes, in one of the hotel reception rooms that faces east and looks down on the ocean.''

The picture came vividly to her. Jesse in a white tuxedo. Herself in a flowing, midi-length, white lace skirt and delicate Victorian-style blouse, a wreath of flowers in her hair. Of course she would ask Ellen to be her maid of honor, and her father would be there to give her away. She would probably end up inviting her mother, stepfather and stepsisters, too.

Hold on, Holly!

For a moment she'd lost sight of the fact that the whole engagement was a fabrication. She'd fallen easily into the fantasy. Too easily!

Joanna broke into Holly's thoughts. "You're smart to keep it small. Big weddings are a hassle. Between the bridal coordinator and Mother...but it's almost over, so I won't complain. I'm just so glad you're here, Jesse." She threw her arms around Jesse again.

Regardless of how the rest of his family felt about him, it was clear that Joanna thought the sun rose and set on her big brother.

Joanna turned to Holly. "I'm glad you're here, too. I hope we get a chance to know each other this week. You must be a special lady to have finally gotten this guy to commit."

"I don't want you monopolizing her too much, JoJo. Holly and I have both taken time off work and plan to spend some time together...alone." His gaze

drifted to the bed. Then he winked at Holly, imply-
ing an intimate secret between the two of them.

Holly managed a smile for Joanna's benefit, but
her pulse was pounding in her ears, and her knees
were wobbly. The image of herself and Jesse in the
bed together was as vivid as the earlier one of the
wedding had been.

*No way, Holly. You haven't hung on to your vir-
ginity this long to give it up on a one-week fling just
because you've met a gorgeous specimen of a man
who knows the way to look at you to send your hormones into orbit.*

She wasn't necessarily holding out for her wedding night; after all, she wasn't going to get married
for a while, if ever. But she wasn't going to treat the
decision lightly, either. She trusted that she would
know when the time was right.

Joanna's voice broke into her thoughts. "I need to
get cleaned up. Will you two be at dinner? Douglas
will be here. The bridesmaids and relatives will start
arriving tomorrow, so it will be the last quiet family
dinner around here for a while."

"Yes, we'll be there," Jesse said.

After a round of goodbyes, Jesse and Holly were
alone once more.

"Your sister seems nice," Holly said.

"She is."

"How can your parents be such monsters and yet
raise two nice kids?"

He was frowning again. "I never said my parents were monsters, although it wouldn't have mattered. Joanna and I spent more time with our nanny than our parents anyway."

Holly remembered they'd been arguing before the interruption. She didn't want to continue, even though it still upset her that he had suspected she might accept his father's offer of money, she also understood the reasons...whether he accepted them or scoffed them off as talk-show psychoanalysis.

A change of subject was in order and a change of scenery was, too, now that she couldn't keep her mind off the bed. "Well, I guess I'll go take a shower and then read about the house."

"Feel free to explore. If you need anything, pick up the phone and dial three."

After Holly left, Jesse walked across the room and looked out the window, taking in the familiar neatly manicured lawn. His old room in the west wing had a similar view.

He'd been able to mask his reaction, but he'd been surprised when the butler had shown him and Holly to their rooms. He hadn't expected to be welcomed back as the prodigal son and ushered to his old room, but he hadn't expected to be exiled to the guest wing.

Keep things in perspective, man. This is merely a ploy of Mimi's to get a rise out of you.

He knew his mother would like nothing more than for him to storm into whatever room she was holding court in and demand to be moved to the family wing.

He wouldn't give her the satisfaction.

The Omaha Room was nice. He was ambivalent about it being so close to Holly's room. He liked the idea of being able to keep a close watch on her, but was her proximity going to be too big a temptation?

He'd decided to accept any offer she made, but his conscience demanded she make the offer of her own free choice—not because he'd seduced her into it. With her right across the hall, would it be a case of easier said than done?

Especially since an actual engaged couple would most likely have filled the free time between their arrival and dinner by sating their other appetites.

Appetites fully roused by tempting hours of Holly being perched behind him on the bike.

Appetites he hadn't filled in a long time.

The bathroom, like the rest of her bedroom was sumptuous. Holly felt decadent as she wrapped one plush, peach towel around her wet hair and used the other to dry her body.

Since the weather had warmed, she put on shorts and a Bike Week tank top. It looked out of place in her surroundings, but what the heck . . . it fit the temperature and the part she was playing for the next week.

After blow-drying her hair, she went into the bedroom, took the book from the nightstand and curled up on the couch in front of the fireplace. The sitting area was similar to the one in Jesse's room. With Florida weather she didn't think the fireplaces would get much use, but they gave the rooms a homeyness they might not otherwise have with the coordinated professional decor.

The book not only covered the history of the house and its assorted periods of development, it chronicled the Tyler family, as well. She was surprised at how interesting the reading was, but then, the people she was reading about had walked the halls of this very house and were Jesse's relatives.

Jesse.

She had to admit that he was the reason she was so interested in the book. Curiosity about what made him tick.

When she'd first learned about his estrangement from his family, she'd pictured him as the underdog in the story, and he'd immediately sparked her empathy and earned her sympathy. But the more she was around him, the more she realized he didn't fit the underdog image. Unless he was covering his real feelings, hiding behind carefully erected facades.

She wondered if she could get past that to the man underneath.

But why should she?

After this week, they wouldn't be seeing each other again.

* * *

At twenty after six, Holly took a final look at her red minidress in the mirror before walking across the room to answer the knock at the door. She expected to find Jesse on the other side. But she'd expected to find him in a suit. Instead he was in jeans, although he had on a cotton dress shirt and a tie.

Was his outfit to annoy his parents? Or were the Tylers the jeans-and-tie sort? Remembering Joanna's formal riding outfit, she would bet it was the former.

"Ready to go downstairs?" he asked.

"Yes. Unless you're having second thoughts."

"Of course not."

"I just thought maybe..."

One brow quirked and his lips turned up in his annoying, but adorable, half smile. "More TV psychology?"

"You're impossible."

"So I've heard."

"I just thought maybe now you've been here awhile, you'd decided you wanted to try to make peace with your family instead of—"

Jesse interrupted her. "Do I look like I'm dressed to make peace?"

No, he didn't look like he was dressed to make peace. He also looked less tense than he had at lunch. As if physically arriving at Lake Wyndham had been half the battle for him.

She stepped into the hallway, closing the door behind her. "Let's go, then."

When they reached the ground floor he tucked her arm over his. She could feel the heat of him beneath her hand. What would it feel like to be pressed close to him and absorb his heat along the length of her body?

Her wayward thoughts were interrupted when they stepped into the living room. A magnificently decorated Christmas tree reached from floor to vaulted ceiling. Its colorful lights twinkled.

"Apparently we're the first ones down," Jesse said as he led her farther into the room.

As if by magic, a uniformed waiter appeared and took their drink orders.

Douglas was the next to arrive. Holly liked the handsome young man immediately. He was as pleasant as Joanna, and was also surprised by the news of Jesse's engagement.

When Jesse's sister walked into the room, Holly could see the love between the soon-to-be-married couple reflected on both their faces. Holly felt a fleeting twinge of envy before reminding herself that she didn't have a significant other in her life by choice.

The four of them chatted until the sound of voices approaching the living room interrupted them. Holly glanced toward the door as a man and woman stepped into the room.

Joanna was across the room to them in no time. "Dad, Mom, guess what?"

Jesse slipped his arm around Holly's waist as they turned to face the door.

The new arrivals looked like the perfect society couple. Fashionably dressed, not a hair out of place. Both looked far younger than they must be to have two grown children.

"Jesse's engaged."

"Really?" The "that's nice, dear" wasn't spoken, but Holly could hear it in the tone of Jesse's mother's voice.

The couple looked in their direction. Holly felt like a specimen in a museum bug collection.

"Don't let them intimidate you," Jesse whispered to her as he gently led her in their direction.

Intimidated? Jesse obviously hadn't been intimidated by his parents or he never would have gotten Yankee off the ground. Holly was sure any woman he chose to marry would be equally unflappable. So she put on her brightest smile.

After exchanging polite introductions with her, neither of Jesse's parents spoke to her or Jesse. Their conversation was directed at Joanna or Douglas. Both of whom made an effort to include Holly and Jesse whenever possible. Most of their discussion revolved around the upcoming wedding.

The same strained atmosphere prevailed once they were at the dinner table.

As the meal drew to a close, during a lull in the conversation, Joanna turned to Holly. "Do you work for Yankee, Holly?"

"No, I work in my dad's tattoo parlor." Holly noticed Jesse's mother's startled gaze dart to her husband. "In fact, that's where I met Jesse."

Mimi Tyler paled and spoke directly to Holly for the first time. "Jesse has a tattoo?"

A spark of mischief flared in Holly. "Don't worry, it's not where anyone will see it. Unless they walk in on him while he's in the shower."

"Why on earth would anyone want a tattoo?" Mimi asked.

While Holly suspected it was a rhetorical question, she answered anyway. "It's a form of artistic expression."

"I suppose you have one, too," Mimi said.

Holly smiled. "I have three."

Mimi gasped and looked to her husband.

"Shall we have coffee in the living room?" the elder Jesse asked.

"I should be getting home. I have to work in the morning," Douglas said.

"And Jesse and I have an appointment to get his tuxedo fitted," Joanna added.

"We'll call it a night, then," Jesse Senior said.

Jesse and Holly made their way to their rooms.

As they turned down the hallway Holly said, "Thanks for the nudge earlier, I almost lost it for a minute when they came into the room."

"You recovered quickly. That was a nice touch claiming I have a tattoo."

She stopped in front of the door to her room. "You don't think it was a bit much?"

"You did good."

"Thanks." She smiled at him.

"Do you really have three tattoos?"

She nodded.

Something flared in his eyes as his gaze worked its way down her body. "Are they visible only if someone walks in on you in the shower?"

"No." They were exposed by certain outfits and when she was in a bikini.

His gaze returned to her face. "No?"

"No." She suspected he was dying to know where they were, but was too much of a gentleman to ask. "See you tomorrow."

Jesse rammed his fist into his pillow again, even though he knew a plumped pillow wasn't going to help him sleep. His imagination kept enticing him with visions of smooth, creamy, female flesh adorned with colorful butterflies and flowers. Holly's tattoos must have been close to showing, the dress hadn't covered much of her.

He finally managed to catch a few hours' sleep, but was far from rested when he and Joanna headed off for their appointment.

"So, how long did you know Holly before you two got engaged?"

"A few months. Why?"

"Well ... she's very beautiful and seems sweet, but..."

"She's not our social equal?"

"Jesse, you know I'm not like that. And frankly I'm hurt you would say that to me."

"Sorry, I didn't get much sleep last night."

"Ah."

"What's that supposed to mean?"

"Oh, just that if you and Holly were up late together, I don't have anything to worry about after all."

Jesse wasn't about to tell her that he hadn't been with Holly. "Could you be a bit more specific, please?"

"Last night it seemed the two of you were a little tentative at times. There's obviously chemistry between you, but you seemed rather cautious for an engaged couple."

"I'm surrounded by amateur psychiatrists." Jesse shook his head. "Would you have been happier if I'd made love to Holly on the dining room table?"

"Of course not." She turned the car into the parking lot at the tuxedo shop.

Jesse made a mental note to talk to Holly about what Joanna had said. Maybe they should spend some time together this afternoon and work at being less "cautious" with each other.

Five

———

Holly decided to keep a low profile while Jesse was out of the house. She didn't think she would do or say anything to make anyone suspect they weren't really engaged, but why take unnecessary chances? She had breakfast brought to her room, then curled up on the couch and worked on fashion sketches, letting her mind wander and her hand take control of the pencil.

Noticing that stars and stripes seemed to be incorporating themselves into the designs, she set out to come up with possible ideas for Yankee. It couldn't hurt to have samples to show Jesse...just in case the subject came up.

As often happened when she was sketching, she lost track of time until she heard Jesse's door open and close. She put her supplies away and was on her way to his room to see what was on the agenda for the afternoon when she heard his door again. Followed by a knock on hers.

Her first thought when she saw him in the hallway was that he hadn't gotten enough sleep.

So, invite him in for a nap.

Good grief, what was getting into her?

She smiled. "Hi. All finished with the tuxedo fitting?"

"All done. Do you feel like going on a picnic?"

The invitation surprised her. "A picnic?"

"Down by the lake."

Picnicking, it seemed, was a routine outing at Lake Wyndham. All it took was a call to the kitchen and a well-stocked basket was ready for them when they arrived downstairs.

Jesse carried the basket with one hand and reached for her with the other. Hand in hand, they headed toward the lake, stopping when they came to a shady spot beneath an oak tree.

During lunch Jesse alternated between charming and preoccupied. Holly matched her responses to whichever tone he set. She was surprised the silences between them were starting to seem companionable, rather than awkward, the more time they spent together.

She was going to mention it to Jesse, to see if he felt the same, but when she looked at him, his eyes were closed. Was he asleep? She looked closer.

He had to be asleep.

See, Holly, he did need a nap.

Even while sleeping, Jesse looked as ruggedly handsome as ever, but there was a softening to the lines around his eyes and mouth that made him look more approachable.

Approachable?

The word repeated in her mind as her gaze lingered on Jesse's mouth. When he smiled, it sent thrills through her. When he frowned, it made her want to do or say something to make him smile. Now that his mouth was softened with sleep, she felt the urge to approach it with her own.

To touch . . . to feel . . . to taste . . .

No way!

She forced her gaze away from the sleeping male and stared at the lake. The water looked inviting, but considering this was Florida, chances were good there might be an alligator lurking beneath the surface. Danger hidden beneath a calm surface.

She glanced at Jesse. The description fit him, too.

Holly spent the next fifteen minutes soaking up the Florida sunshine and watching a horse, the color of rich mahogany, frolic in a nearby pasture. A shiver worked its way along her spine moments before Jesse's hand closed around hers.

She turned and looked at him. "Welcome back."

He yawned and sat up, stretching his arms. "We need to enjoy the peace and quiet now. From what Joanna said, her bridal party and the first wave of family will be here by dinner."

"Cocktails at six-thirty and dinner at seven again?"

"Yes, and I think we need to discuss our relationship before we face the crowd. Joanna mentioned that we seemed cautious with each other. Maybe we could touch more."

"We held hands off and on last night. And you had your arm around me when you introduced me to your parents. What should we do differently?"

"I want you to flirt with me."

Holly fluttered her eyelashes. "Like this?"

Jesse laughed.

Holly knew how to flirt. She also knew flirting could sometimes be dangerous. "If I flirt, you won't think I'm coming on to you?"

"Of course not. No more than my kissing you means I'm coming on to you."

His words registered about the same time he moved his mouth onto hers. His lips were hard, warm, and insistent in their pursuit and Holly felt as if the ground beneath her had turned to quicksand. It briefly crossed her mind that she should protest, but it felt too good. It was obviously something he'd had lots of practice at, so she left the lead to him and followed.

Followed when he deepened the kiss by nudging her lips apart with his tongue. Followed when he shifted to cradle her in his arms.

Followed until, at the sound of someone clearing their throat, Jesse broke the connection between them.

Slightly bemused, Holly turned to see Joanna and Douglas standing by the edge of the blanket.

"Sorry to interrupt, but Doug and I are going horseback riding and wondered if you two would care to join us."

"I don't," Jesse said. "You can go if you'd like," he told Holly.

"I think I'll pass, too."

A brief conversation followed, but Holly let it go on around her as she focused on the sensation of being held in Jesse's arms and thinking about the kiss. A first kiss was usually a tentative, experimental connecting of lips. Their first kiss had been a knock-your-socks-off, turbo-charged explosion.

After the other couple went on their way, Holly scooted off his lap and across the blanket until they were no longer touching. She took a deep breath and let it out slowly.

Jesse ran one hand through his hair. "You can say that again."

Could the kiss have affected Jesse as much as it had her?

When she looked at him, she could see that it had. That rattled her almost as much as the kiss itself.

Jesse leaned back, resting on his elbows. "I hope that lacked enough caution for Joanna."

It took a moment for the full meaning of his statement to sink in.

He'd known Joanna was there. The kiss had been for her benefit.

Holly should have expected something like that. After all, he'd said the kiss didn't mean he was coming on to her.

She wondered about the women he *did* come on to. How they felt. Knowing he could have his pick of almost any woman he wanted, it must feel incredibly exciting to know he'd chosen you.

"Would you like to have the rest of the afternoon off, so to speak, or would you like to do something together? Swimming or sailing, maybe?"

"Which seems most appropriate for an engaged couple?"

Jesse smiled. "I'd say nine out of ten engaged couples would opt for some time between the sheets."

"And the tenth?"

"There's the stable, gazebo, swimming pool—"

"You can stop anytime. I get the general idea." And the part of her that had enjoyed his kiss so much wanted to holler, *Let's go for it*. Instead she asked, "What would you do this afternoon if I wasn't here?"

"I'd take the bike out for a run."

Holly had sketches she could work on and the book about the house she could read. Either would occupy her time without torturing her senses. There was no reason she should volunteer to spend the afternoon pressed against him from shoulder to knee. No reason at all.

But instead of accepting his offer of the afternoon off, she said, "Let's take the bike out for a run then."

Holly told herself someone might be watching out the window, so once seated behind Jesse, she wrapped her arms around him, clasping her gloved hands together. The result was that she was pressed even closer to him than she'd been on the ride to Lake Wyndham.

Next week would be business as usual, so she forced herself to relax and enjoy.

She enjoyed more than she relaxed, but what the heck, she was only human. And when a human female is in close proximity to an incredibly sexy male, it was only natural for her to be affected. "Survival of the fittest" depended on that kind of thing. Who was she to challenge Mother Nature?

They rode to the east coast. Once there, they had ice tea at a small oceanside café then set off for a stroll along the beach.

"Douglas seems like a nice guy. Has your sister known him long?"

"Several years. They met in college."

"Have you ever been married?"

"Have *I* ever been married?" Jesse frowned. "Is that any of your business?"

"Probably not, but I was just making conversation. If I really wanted to know, I'm sure a trip to the library would get me the answer."

"You're right. Most of my private life is an open book. So in answer to your question, no. I've never been married."

"Why not?" The question was out before she could stop it. "I know it isn't any of my business." And it was the kind of information she wouldn't likely find in back issues of newspapers and magazines.

Jesse responded with a question of his own. "Why aren't you married?"

"I told you before, the only guy I would marry would be Santa Claus. And he hasn't asked yet."

"But you didn't say why."

"Because he's kind, considerate and stable. I don't want to play mind games with some hotshot who thinks he's God's gift to women."

He nodded. "I get it. A bad relationship in your past."

"No, just what I learned by watching my friends and listening to the guys in the tattoo parlor talk about women. But what about you? You didn't answer my question about why you've never married."

Holly was beginning to think he wasn't going to when he spoke. "I haven't fallen in love."

Holly's steps slowed. "I was expecting to hear a dark tale of heartbreak from your past. Something to explain why you run hot and cold, and why sometimes you're downright grouchy."

Jesse laughed. "This is the first time a woman has told me to my face that she thinks I'm grouchy. Apparently you don't go for the strong, silent type."

"The moody, brooding type? No."

"I should have known that. Since Santa is neither moody nor brooding."

Holly sighed. "I must be missing something, because I just don't get it. You're handsome, sexy as sin, rich, powerful. You walk into a room and women's heads turn. You should be the happiest guy on earth. But you're not, and I have to wonder what gives."

"And you can go right on wondering."

"Because it's none of my business. You're a broken record, sweetcheeks."

"Sweetcheeks?" He laughed again.

And Holly couldn't help smiling. "What's the matter, Jess, no one ever call you sweetcheeks, either?"

Jesse stopped walking. Reaching out, he took hold of her, turning her until she stood in front of him. He draped his arms loosely over her shoulders.

"No one's ever called me grouchy, sweetcheeks or Jess."

Holly could see sparks of amusement in his eyes as his gaze met hers. Then he looked at her lips.

She met him halfway. There was nothing tentative about this kiss, either. It was instant sparks and fireworks. She melted from the heat, leaning into him for support.

No doubt about it, this guy was some kisser. He gave his all to their make-believe engagement. She wasn't sure who he'd spotted on the beach, someone from the house, or some other acquaintance, but whoever it was wouldn't have any reason to describe their behavior toward each other as "cautious."

Jesse slid one hand beneath her hair, feathering his fingertips across the bare skin of her nape. He moved his other arm around her waist and used it to pull her lower body more tightly into him.

Her breath caught in her throat. Even through the sensual haze his kisses had woven around her, she was able to recognize the source of the hardness wedged between them. As if by some inborn instinct, she sighed and nuzzled closer.

Long moments later Jesse placed a few last kisses at the edges of her swollen lips. Holly straightened and looked around.

Except for the two of them, the beach was deserted.

"Holly, what are you looking for?"

"I'm checking to see whose benefit that was for."

"It wasn't for anyone's benefit. Except mine and yours."

She looked at him. "But...why?"

"Because it felt so good the first time."

Jesse watched the palm trees on the horizon disappear from his sideview mirrors. Their walk on the beach had been interesting.

What was it with this woman?

At times he felt a peace and comfort being with her that he rarely felt around other people. She gave him a feeling that he could be himself and that would be all right with her. There seemed to be no pressure on him to impress her or live up to her expectations. Of course, she was being paid for being with him, but he had a hunch she might act the same way regardless.

And it was fun watching her sparkle and shine—to sit back and observe her obvious enjoyment of life. *Joie de vivre.* His high school French teacher had had a banner hanging above the doorway. Jesse hadn't thought about it in years. The phrase, meaning a buoyant enjoyment of life, hadn't seemed to fit any of the tormented teenage students that shuffled beneath it, but it fit Holly to a T.

Holly enjoyed life. And he enjoyed being around her. Except when she got into one of her moods where she wanted to pry into his private life. Although he didn't get the feeling she was prying with the same morbid curiosity—the fascination with a Yankee Hunk that drove most of the women who approached him—that kept the tabloids in business.

One thing he was crystal clear on, kissing her was an experience. Now that he'd had her in his arms and tasted her, he wondered how he was going to be able to keep his hands off her. He was sure she would make love with the same wholehearted enthusiasm she invested in all her activities.

Touching her this evening, with the wedding company as chaperons, was going to be sweet torture. He would be able to touch her in ways it was acceptable for an engaged couple to touch.

But what about when the two of them were alone, without someone around to make sure he didn't overstep polite boundaries and slip his hands underneath her clothes to touch the warm female body beneath?

Oh, how he wanted to. Wanted to curve his fingers around her full breasts, tease her nipples with his thumbs until they hardened and she moaned with pleasure.

Just the thought of it was making his jeans uncomfortably tight.

Back at the house Holly found herself missing Jesse once they went their separate ways to get ready for dinner. Maybe she did like the strong, silent type after all. Or maybe it was the lure of the challenge to break through his reserve that appealed to her.

She'd made a small hole in it, or so she assumed after the way he'd kissed her at the beach. The kiss had been purely voluntary, and not part of the roles they were playing.

When Jesse arrived at the door to escort her to dinner, he was wearing a suit.

"No rebel clothes?" she asked.

"I don't want to become a cliché."

She understood the feeling. After all, she was spending the week as a cliché of a biker chick. That's what he was paying her to do.

Throughout the evening, Jesse kept Holly close to his side. She flirted with him, smiled, sent smoldering glances, and touched him whenever circumstances allowed. He did the same.

While she was well aware that it was all for show, her traitorous body wasn't. It joined forces with her imagination and wreaked all kinds of havoc.

At dinner there was an assortment of Tyler uncles, aunts and cousins and Joanna's bridal attendants present, as well as Douglas's and Jesse's parents.

Jesse's parents greeted her by name. It seemed stuffy of them to call their future daughter-in-law Ms. Bryant, but at least they got her name right. She had to give them credit for that.

Two of the four bridesmaids and the maid of honor did their best to capture Jesse's attention, but while he was polite, he made it clear he and Holly were an item and he was not available.

She also noticed that any time one of the men looked in her direction, Jesse would touch her. Small gestures, such as a hand on hers, a touch on the arm, a gentle squeeze of the shoulder.

When the talk at the table turned to polo, Jesse quietly filled her in on the terminology being used.

He was doing a great job at this acting stuff. If she didn't know better, she could almost believe they were a happily engaged couple herself.

After dinner the younger members of the party went into the living room to string popcorn for the Christmas tree. She and Jesse sat close together on the couch.

They didn't stay too long before Jesse said their good-nights and walked her to her room. Holly tried to mentally will someone to appear in the hallway, prompting Jesse to kiss her. But they remained alone, and he left her with just a platonic "Good night."

It was probably for the best. His kisses left her yearning for more. In the interest of a good night's sleep, kissing Jesse was definitely something to avoid.

Holly got ready for bed, then settled in to finish reading the book about the house.

She'd read a few pages when she heard what sounded like someone knocking on Jesse's door. Quietly, she went to investigate, opening her door just far enough so she could peek out.

One of the bridesmaids, Darlene, dressed in a slinky something halfway between hostess wear and sleepwear, was standing in front of Jesse's door with a bottle of champagne in one hand and two glasses in the other.

As Holly watched, the door opened a few inches.

Darlene held up the bottle. "I thought we could have a toast for old time's sake."

"You didn't have enough to drink at dinner?"

"So all your attention wasn't on your little friend, after all."

"Holly is my fiancée."

"Well, you're not married yet, and rumor has it you have separate rooms." She pushed her shoulder against the door. It remained in place until Darlene started to slide slowly downward as if she was feeling faint. Jesse opened the door and caught her before she reached the ground. She held the bottle close to her chest and wrapped her other arm limply around his neck.

The last thing Holly saw before the couple disappeared in the direction of the sitting area was the glitter of two crystal glasses framed against a tanned back.

Now what?

Jesse had left the door open, so she doubted he had any intention of taking the other woman up on her obvious offer, and no doubt he could probably handle the situation on his own, but the ordeal would be shorter if she gave him a helping hand.

Holly flipped off her bedroom light and slipped into the hallway, closing her door quietly. She tiptoed into Jesse's room.

The champagne and the glasses were on the coffee table. Jesse stood next to it, an amazingly recovered Darlene clinging to him.

"Gee, I hope I'm not interrupting anything."

Darlene slid her arms down and took a few steps back. "Jesse and I haven't seen each other in a long time, so I thought we could discuss old times."

Holly shrugged. "I see. Well, discuss quietly please, I'm exhausted." She blew Jesse a kiss, walked across the room and crawled into his bed. Snuggling into the pillows, she closed her eyes. It was a struggle not to let her imagination have a field day with images of what could happen if Jesse was there in the bed with her.

Luckily she didn't have long to wait before Darlene left in a snit, slamming the door behind her.

Holly climbed out of bed. She pulled the covers up and smoothed them into place.

"That's not necessary. I'll be getting in there myself soon."

She turned. Jesse was leaning against the back of the couch. His gaze roamed slowly down her body.

Holly caught her bottom lip between her teeth as she stood quietly through the ordeal. She watched heat flare in his eyes as his gaze lingered on her breasts and she heard the quick intake of breath when his perusal dropped below the hem of her cropped T-shirt. She knew the white lace of her panties gave a shadowy peek of flat stomach and strawberry-blond curls.

But, dang it all, she'd dressed for curling up in bed alone, not for running around rescuing hunks from over-amorous females.

Six

_____

"**Y**ou have a holly tattoo." Jesse's voice was a harsh whisper.

The tattoo was over her right hipbone, just above the lacy elastic of her underwear. "You're right."

"That's one."

"One?"

"You said you had three tattoos."

Holly started to plant her hands on her hips, then realized the gesture would emphasize her breasts even more. Her breasts felt different somehow—heavier, swollen, tingly. "This isn't an art show, pal. So pop your gorgeous green peeps back into their sockets. I came in here to do you a favor."

She started for the door. When she got there, she heard voices—one male, one female—in the hallway. They were approaching from the direction of the stairs and stopped to linger not long after passing Jesse's door. From the sound of things, they seemed in no hurry to go into their rooms.

"We have a slight problem," she whispered. "There's a couple in the hallway."

Jesse came to stand next to her. He listened.

Holly took the opportunity to feast her eyes on the well-defined muscles and the sprinkling of dark hair on his naked chest. Man, was he ever gorgeous. Not just a hunk, but a hunk and a half.

He swore softly, pulling her attention from his oh-so-close, oh-so-tempting body and back to the matter at hand—the couple in the hallway.

"Well," he said quietly, "she'll either break down and invite him in or he'll take the hint and leave. We've got a bottle of champagne. Would you like a drink?"

I'd rather have a kiss.

A step forward, some cooperation from Jesse, and she would have the kiss. Instead she stepped back. "I'll pass, but I would like to sit down." She headed for the couch, trying not to think about the inviting bed she'd just climbed out of.

"Holly?"

She turned.

"No insult intended, but would you mind wearing my bathrobe?"

He was doing that sexy once-over thing again, as if trying to memorize every inch of her before it was hidden from view, even though he was the one suggesting she cover up.

"All right. Where is it?"

"Where's what?"

"Your bathrobe."

Jesse shook his head as if to clear it, then turned and headed toward the closet.

When he returned, he had a shirt for himself as well as a black silk robe. Holly slipped the robe on, deliberately avoiding looking at him until after she'd tied it closed. She sat on the couch, pulling her legs up to tuck her feet within the soft folds.

Jesse joined her. He sat well to his own side, but he was gazing intently at a strand of hair that hung over her shoulder to curl against the dark, shiny fabric. He let out his breath in a rush of air, then leaned back, putting his bare feet on the coffee table.

The man even had sexy toes! Was there no justice?

A man so totally sexy was probably used to having a lot of sex. In fact, he'd probably be doing it right now, at this minute, if she hadn't interrupted him. But they were supposed to be engaged. Wouldn't a fiancée have thwarted Darlene's little visit?

"I hope I didn't step out of line and ruin your plans for the evening.... I mean ... you did want to be rescued, didn't you?"

Jesse moved his gaze from her hair. "I wouldn't have slept with her, if that's what you're getting at."

"Well, I wasn't sure. After all, you are actually single. Even though we are engaged. Sort of engaged," she clarified.

"In everyone else's eyes, we *are* engaged. I intend to act accordingly."

A warm, cozy feeling settled over her. She felt cherished and special. As though Jesse's avowal of fidelity was really being made to her, Holly Bryant, woman. Not Holly Bryant, paid fiancée stand-in.

But then Jesse continued. "I expect you to do the same if any of the other men make a pass at you. From the looks some of them were giving you, be on your guard. They might do just that."

She already knew about his pattern of not trusting people, but his remark still annoyed her. Instead of sloughing it off, she glared at him. "Ah, shucks, sweetcheeks! You mean I can't use this trip to try and catch me a rich husband?"

"A wife is the last thing these guys will be looking for."

"Your soon-to-be brother-in-law, Douglas, obviously was looking for a wife," she countered.

"What happened to your fervent pledge to marry Santa Claus?"

Holly snapped her fingers. "You're right. Thanks for reminding me. I guess it's just as well, then, that any guy who comes on to me isn't looking for a wife."

"Since we're supposed to be engaged, I'll expect you not to give them what they *are* looking for. If you do find yourself tempted, come to me and I'll remedy the situation for you."

Holly felt the blood rushing to her cheeks. Did he mean what she thought he did? "You'll remedy the *situation?*"

"Holly, I understand about a woman's needs and if some guy comes on to you and in the process gets you all hot and bothered—"

The only one getting her hot and bothered was him! And at the moment, it wasn't in a sexual way. "You're offering to sleep with me?"

"I'm offering to have sex with you."

"That's quite a noble sacrifice you're willing to make, Jess. It might even get you nominated for a humanitarian award."

He moved his feet to the floor, scooted closer to her, and slid one arm across the back of the couch. "Not really. I intend to take pleasure of my own at the same time I give you your relief."

Suddenly "hot and bothered" shifted from angry to the other—the sexual kind he'd offered to help with. Holly stood and walked to the fireplace. Crossing her arms over her chest, she rubbed her hands back and forth across the cool fabric of the overlong sleeves. His offer frightened yet intrigued her.

For a moment as she remembered the sight of Jesse shirtless, she wished she was the type of woman who could throw caution to the wind—indulge herself. "That's an interesting seduction line you have there."

"I don't have a seduction line."

"Never needed one?"

He leaned deeper into the cushions and put his feet on the table. "That's right."

"You just crook your little finger and they fall on their backs?"

He smiled, a slow, devilish smile. "It depends what I'm in the mood for."

Holly had never had sex, but she knew there could be more to it than the woman on her back and she mentally kicked herself for setting herself up for his suggestive retort.

A retort that conjured all sorts of images in her mind. Seductively tempting images. She wondered if Jesse would make such a calm, straightforward offer if he knew she was a virgin. No, he'd most likely use an entirely different approach, something smooth.

She was sure he could be as smooth as the dark fabric she was wrapped in. So why would he sit back and wait for some other guy to get her turned on and then step in for the main event?

It couldn't be that he didn't want her physically. From their kiss on the beach she knew he did. Was he holding back because of what she'd asked the day he'd offered her the job? About whether he expected her to sleep with him?

A disturbing thought entered her mind. Maybe for some perverse reason he enjoyed finishing what another man started. It would probably be wisest to change the subject, but she couldn't help asking, "Why would you want to take a woman to bed who had just gotten hot and bothered in some other man's arms?"

"Would it be so different from taking a woman to bed who's all hot and bothered from staring at a billboard or magazine ad?" There was a bitter edge to his voice.

An uneasy feeling settled in her midsection. She walked over and sat next to Jesse. "That's happened to you, hasn't it?"

There were shadows in his eyes when he looked at her. His smile was tight. "Being a sex symbol is no day at the beach."

His words seemed to slough off and make light of things, but Holly could feel the hurt and pain behind them. Her own discomfort about his offer to her was forgotten in her concern for Jesse.

Before she could think of something appropriate to say, he continued. "Women have asked me to wear that damned red leather outfit I wore in the photo to make love to them."

Holly was puzzled. She'd seen the ad, of course. And sure he looked killer in the red leather pants, jacket, knee-high boots and visored helmet that he'd worn in the ad, but he looked even better in a pair of faded blue jeans, his handsome face uncovered. Frankly, if the two of them made love, she would want him in nothing but a smile. "I don't understand why."

"I do. They've fallen under a spell. Bought into the fantasy image created by our ad agency. Bought into the Yankee Hunk mystique." He ran his hands through his hair. "It's great for business, gets us plenty of publicity, which in turn helps us sell bikes, but it's ruined my social life and is absolute hell on my libido."

"It's natural for there to be some women who go groupie on you. All celebrities have fans." She still wasn't convinced all the attention wasn't a major ego booster for him. Then again... "Now that I think about it. I can understand how you would need more from a relationship than hero worship."

"It's not just that *I* need more. When they come seeking the fantasy, I can't give them what they need, either. I'm just a man."

Didn't he realize that saying he was just a man was like saying Mount Everest was just a molehill? "You've got to lighten up. You're a major hunk, Jess. Even without the billboard thing, being around you might be intimidating for some women."

"You haven't had any problems."

If he only knew.

There was the sound of a door closing and footsteps heading toward the stairs. Holly breathed a deep sigh of relief.

She stood, stretching. "If they'd stayed up any later, I might have fallen asleep right here."

Jesse laughed. "Was my sparkling conversation that dull?"

"I didn't mean—"

"Settle down, Holly. I'm teasing."

Of course he'd been teasing. There was laughter in his eyes. But as she watched, sparks of something else joined it.

"I guess I'll leave now," Holly said, but made no attempt to follow through, frozen in place by the desire in Jesse's eyes.

"You could stay. The bed's big enough for two."

She turned, not giving herself even a moment to be tempted. "Ah, no thanks."

There was a light tapping on the door. Holly looked over her shoulder to Jesse. "Expecting someone?"

He shook his head, then glanced toward the bed. Holly took it as a hint. She crossed the room and climbed beneath the covers again. Once she was settled, Jesse opened the door.

Watching through her eyelashes, Holly saw another of Joanna's bridesmaids in the hallway.

"Isn't it a little late for visiting, April?"

"I saw the light under your door."

"I'm getting ready to turn in. In fact Holly's already asleep." He nodded toward the bed.

"Holly?"

"My fiancée. You met at dinner."

"But I heard you two had separate rooms."

Holly wondered who else had checked into Jesse's rooming arrangements and might be stopping by for a visit. She closed her eyes and gave in to the invitation of the bed to relax. Jesse's and April's voices continued, but Holly wasn't listening to the words.

As she snuggled against the pillow slip, she realized a faint trace of Jesse's after-shave lingered in the fabric.

When the door clicked shut, she opened her eyes and scooted to sit up with her back against the headboard.

Jesse walked to the bed and sat on the edge, even with her hip. "Guess I owe you another thanks for rescuing me again."

"Will you be safe the rest of the night?"

And what about tomorrow? And the days, and nights, after that?

He shrugged. "Your guess is as good as mine."

"I'll try to listen for any noises from here."

"You could just stay." He held his hands up, palms outward, to ward off any protest. "One of us can sleep in the bed, the other can have the couch. There are extra blankets and sheets in the closet."

Holly yawned. It had been a long day and she was tired. If she went back to her own room, she would be straining, trying to be alert to any noise from Jesse's room. She would have a much more restful sleep if she accepted his offer to stay. But if he got too close to her she was afraid she would be tempted to accept his earlier offer—the one about providing relief.

"If I stay, I want your promise that the sleeping areas will stay separate."

"I promise to stay in my own space. Unless, of course, you invite me into yours."

Would you like that invitation in writing? "Since I'm already in the bed, you can be first to try out the couch." She snuggled down, rolled over to her side and closed her eyes.

Holly intended to fall asleep right away. Instead she ended up listening. Listening as Jesse got the couch ready. Listening to the sound of water running while he showered.

In her mind she could see the droplets cascading over him. Touching him as she longed to let her fingers touch him. She turned over, trying to ignore the image. But it wouldn't be ignored. It tortured her even after the water was shut off.

She wondered what Jesse was planning to wear to sleep and whether her being there would influence his choice in any way. She was still wearing his robe. Should she offer it to him? No, she would need it in the morning.

Morning. It seemed so far away...

* * *

The aroma of coffee and bacon crept through the fog of sleep surrounding Holly. Slowly she opened her eyes. Jesse was having breakfast at a small table by the window. A covered plate sat across from him.

Almost as if he sensed her looking at him, he turned and caught her gaze. "Good morning."

"Good morning. How did breakfast get here?"

"I had it brought up. I took the liberty of ordering for you."

"Thanks." She sat up, threading her hands through her hair, hoping it would fall into some semblance of order. "They were sure quiet. I didn't hear a thing."

Jesse took a sip of coffee. "Some chaperone you are. Half a dozen women could have snuck in and had their wicked way with me and I would have been completely at their mercy."

Holly was sure the reason she'd been so deeply asleep was that it had been such a struggle to get to sleep in the first place. She'd been so aware of Jesse's nearness, she was lucky to have slept at all.

Jesse set down his cup and picked up his fork. "Come and eat before it gets cold."

Holly joined him at the table. She realized this was the first time she'd had breakfast alone with a man other than her father. Jesse was fully dressed, and they'd slept on opposite sides of the room, but the fact that she was wearing his bathrobe lent a certain intimacy to the occasion.

She lifted the cover off her plate and set it to the side. For a while they ate in silence, then Holly asked, "What are we doing today?"

"Joanna called this morning and invited you to a luncheon she's throwing for her bridesmaids. I told her you'd let her know."

She'd slept through the phone ringing, too! She must have been more exhausted than she'd thought. "Do you think I should go?"

"If we were actually engaged, would you want to go?"

If she and Joanna were really going to become sisters-in-law, she would welcome the chance to spend time with the other woman and her friends. "Probably."

"Then I think you should go."

The luncheon was held in a private dining room at the Lake Wyndham Country Club. Other than Darlene and April, who said little more to her than hello, the rest of the bridesmaids were friendly toward Holly, and she had a nice time.

When she got to the house she found that her clothes and personal belongings had been moved into Jesse's room. At least she wouldn't have to worry about sneaking across the hallway in Jesse's bathrobe as she'd done this morning, but there was something unsettling about seeing her clothes hanging in the closet side by side with his.

Her gaze drifted toward the bed. She pictured the two of them sleeping side by side in it. Side by side, replete after having exhausted themselves in more intimate positions.

Her daydream was interrupted by the sound of the door opening. Blood rushed to her cheeks as she turned to find Jesse standing in the doorway. She reminded herself there was no way he could know what she'd been thinking and started to smile, then stopped when she noticed he was frowning.

He closed the door and walked toward her. "I can't believe you told them I cried watching *Old Yeller!*"

Holly bit the inside of her bottom lip to keep from laughing. Once the urge had passed she said, "They were all comparing stories about why they'd fallen in love with Skip, Biff or whichever preppie they're infatuated with at the moment, so I had to tell about the moment I fell in love with you."

"You would fall in love over a few tears during a G-rated movie? Couldn't you have said you'd fallen for my sexual prowess or what was it you called them last night... my 'gorgeous green peeps'?"

"I could have, but I went with the first thing that came to mind. I think it's incredibly sexy for a man to be able to honestly express his more tender feelings openly."

Jesse looked toward the ceiling and shook his head. "You want honest emotion. How's this?" He looked at Holly. "It really ticks me off to have bimbos like Darlene and April laughing at me for something I didn't do."

"That's emotion, but I don't think it's completely honest. I think you're more embarrassed than angry. I'll bet you did cry at *Old Yeller.*"

"I did not cry."

"I'll bet you felt like crying."

"No, it was a movie. If it were the same situation in real life, I might feel like crying, but not for a movie."

Holly started to open her mouth to speak, but Jesse held up his hand to stop her. "So, for the record, I'm not embarrassed, I'm angry. And for your information, a man can have tender feelings, be perfectly capable of expressing them openly in the appropriate situation and *not* cry over movies."

He turned and stalked to the closet. After grabbing his leather jacket, he left the room, slamming the door behind him.

Turning out of the driveway onto the small country road, Jesse gunned the Yankee's engine and took off with a roar. He let the wind rush over him and the blur of passing scenery absorb his attention.

Mile after mile, he let the distance between himself and Holly grow.

Holly and her damned holly tattoo, not to mention the other two he hadn't seen but fantasized about searching for. The sight of her climbing out of his bed last night, wearing next to nothing had almost been too much for him.

He'd almost abandoned his good intentions of letting her decide whether they became lovers or not by tumbling her right back into his bed.

And ever since he'd let the moment pass, he'd been doubting his sanity.

Seeing her in his bathrobe had been sweet torture, too. Her hair looked as striking against black silk as he'd imagined it would.

It was true, he wasn't one to cry at movies. But since Holly had pretended that was the moment she'd fallen in love with him, it must be something she considered important in a man.

He'd bet Santa wouldn't cry over a movie, either.

Besides, it shouldn't matter to him what Holly deemed ideal in a man, let alone bother him that he didn't fit her profile of the perfect man.

It shouldn't make any difference.

So, why did it?

Seven

Holly was ready to go down for dinner and was beginning to think she was going to be on her own when Jesse returned from wherever he'd stormed off to. From his windblown appearance, she guessed that he'd been for a motorcycle ride.

"Give me ten minutes to get ready," he said.

"No problem."

He was ready in eight. Still wearing motorcycle boots and blue jeans, he'd changed into a gray Henley shirt with Yankee embroidered in red. His choice complemented the denim skirt and jacket she was wearing with a red leather bustier.

Nothing was said about the argument they'd had that afternoon.

With even more prewedding guests on hand, dinner was served buffet style. After they filled their plates, Jesse led Holly to the screened patio and over to one of the small candlelit tables set around the swimming pool.

Jesse was more talkative this evening. As they ate, he quietly amused Holly with anecdotes about the various relatives milling around.

She was having a nice time, until she remembered it was all pretend. The whole friendly act was for show. The whole week was for show. She knew that up front. There'd been no subterfuge between the two of them. So why did the thought of it being make-believe suddenly leave her feeling unsettled and annoyed?

Because Jesse was playing his part so well?

He was playing it so well that everyone seemed to accept them as a couple. Although his parents weren't falling over themselves to be ultrafriendly and had seemed put off by the talk of tattoos that first night, they seemed accepting of her, too.

"You know, your family doesn't seem to have a problem with your being here."

He glanced around. "That surprises me. I expected to be more persona non grata than I have been."

"So did I."

"I knew they wouldn't be openly rude to you, but I did expect a serious effort to break us up."

"After the way you stuck to your guns about motorcycles, maybe your parents realize they would be wasting their time trying to influence you on anything else."

"It's possible. But I'm not convinced enough to let my guard down."

"It's probably best never to let your guard down when dealing with difficult parents."

Jesse looked more intently at her. "You're referring to your mother?"

"Yes." Holly nodded. "She never threatened me or gave me an ultimatum the way your parents did, but she occasionally goes on super-mom rampages where she tries to turn me into a proper role model for my stepsisters. And proper to Mother means turtlenecks on all but the warmest days."

Jesse's gaze wandered downward, lingering where the curves of her breasts were pushed above the red leather of her bustier. His hands curled into loose fists, as though he was fighting the urge to reach across the table and touch. "Putting you in a turtleneck should be against the law."

Holly fought the temptation to take his hand and place it against her skin.

"Is that a compliment, Jess?"

"Fishing for one?"

No, she wasn't fishing for a compliment, but it was suddenly important to her that she know whether Jesse found her attractive. She was afraid to consider the reasons why. "No, just wondering if you like what you're seeing."

"Come on, Holly. You don't need me to tell you you're beautiful."

"Beauty is a matter of taste." And even his offer to take her to bed didn't necessarily mean he thought she was beautiful. "Some men find me beautiful. That doesn't mean you do."

"I do. Believe me, I do."

The heat of his gaze took her breath away.

"Hey, you two, enough with the goo-goo eyes." Joanna's arrival was like a drenching with cold water. "Come into the sitting room. We're going to play bridge."

Jesse folded his napkin and set it on the table next to his plate. "Actually, I was about to take Holly to see the rose garden."

A smile tugged at the corner of Joanna's lips. "In the dark?"

"There's a full moon."

Strolling through the rose garden in the moonlight? Holly wasn't sure she wanted any part of it.

No, that wasn't true.

The frightening truth was that she wanted *every* part of it. That was why she was feeling unsettled and why she wanted Jesse to find her attractive. She wanted to walk hand-in-hand with Jesse, letting the romantic setting be more than just a ploy to convince other people the two of them were lovers.

"Oh, all right," Joanna conceded. "I'll see you two later, then. Or should I say, see you tomorrow?" She moved on to the next table.

Jesse stood and held out his hand to Holly. She placed hers in it, and he wove their fingers together. In silence they left the patio and walked along the flagstone path toward the far side of the house. Their way was lit by the moon and the lights strategically placed within the planted borders.

They reached the rose garden. The flower beds circled outward from a fountain in the center. Paved footpaths ran alongside each bed and four slightly larger paths, at ninety-degree angles, led from the outermost flower beds to the fountain.

The only sounds were their footsteps and the rain-like patter of water in the fountain. The fragrance of roses hung heavy in the air. Holly took a deep breath and let it out on a sigh.

Jesse slowed, then stopped and turned her to face him. "Holly, I'm sorry about the way I acted this afternoon. I was out of line."

"I hope you realize I didn't say what I did at the luncheon to make you look bad. It really was just the first thing that came to mind when I tried to imagine falling in love."

But if she had to answer the same question again, she might be tempted to describe a moment like this one. She'd never been in love. The closest she'd been to what she assumed love felt like was now. The contentment of being with Jesse. The joy at having the discord between them settled. The tingling awareness of the warm male standing half a step away. The strong urge to close the distance and press tightly against him.

He reached out and tucked a strand of hair behind her ear, then rested his large hand against her cheek. "Did you fall in love watching *Old Yeller?*"

A strange fluttery feeling swept through her. "No. I've never fallen in love."

Was that really true? Or would it be more correct to say, I've never fallen in love until now?

Jesse's answer was a noncommittal sound and the lowering of his head to move his lips onto hers.

Holly took the step she'd been considering and he welcomed her into his arms and pulled her even closer. His kiss started as a gentle coaxing, but switched to hot and demanding as she responded. She parted her lips, and he added the seductive play of his tongue against hers to the raging storm.

An achy, throbbing need built deep within her. Instinctively she rocked her hips against Jesse, not realizing the full implication of her action until he moved his hands down and held her still, pulling her close, making her aware of his need.

He ended the kiss. They were both breathing as though they'd run a marathon. Holly felt sure her heart was going to beat its way right out of her chest.

Jesse loosened his grip and slowly slid his hands to her waist. Her jacket opened wider. His gaze lowered.

With one finger, he pushed her jacket open even farther. "A hummingbird."

Holly glanced at the small delicate bird tattooed low on the outer swell of her left breast. "That's Humbert."

"Humbert?"

"Yes." A shaky whisper was all she could manage.

Slowly, Jesse traced the artwork. The smooth, deliberate motion made Holly suck in her breath. With his other hand, he tilted her chin up until her gaze met his. He moved his finger down, slipping it beneath red leather and zeroing in to tease and tantalize the sensitive peak.

She closed her eyes, afraid he might see how much she wanted him and how confused she was about what she was feeling. He shifted, then brushed his lips over her temple, following with a trail of kisses along the side of her neck and down farther until he reached her tattoo. His breath was warm against her bare skin, his lips moist. If only the leather barrier was gone so she could experience the feel of his mouth engulfing the taut bud his expert touch had created.

Jesse straightened and started to lower his lips to hers once again, then pulled back and stepped away. "Holly, I don't know how much more of this I can take." He ran his hands through his hair. "I can't gaze at you over a candlelit table, hold you, kiss you, touch your breasts and feel them respond to me, then sleep on opposite sides of the same room from you.''

"It isn't easy on me, either.''

"Maybe you should move to your own room. Or maybe I should send you home.''

"Or maybe you should take me upstairs and make love to me.'' She was shocked not only by the words, but by how confident and sure her voice sounded when she said them.

Jesse smiled. ''I thought you'd never ask.''

Before she knew it, they were in his room and she was once again in his arms with his lips working their magic. His hands entered the play, too, but instead of teasing and caressing, he used them to strip away the barriers of her clothing until she was uncovered from the waist up.

He leaned her back, and she felt what she had so desperately yearned for earlier in the garden—the satiny warmth of his mouth closing around the tight pink tip of her breast.

She held back a cry of pleasure, but only managed to partially restrain it. The resulting sound vibrated from somewhere deep within her. Jesse answered with tender nibbles and quick flicks of his tongue.

When she had recovered enough to take control of her muscles, Holly reached for the bottom of Jesse's shirt and worked it upward. Heat radiated from him, as if she was holding her hands next to a warm oven, and curling hair tickled her palms.

Once she'd gone as far as she could without his cooperation, Jesse pulled back with a sigh of satisfaction and helped her remove his shirt. She'd seen him without it before, but not this close and not when circumstances allowed her to touch. After rubbing her hands slowly across him, she slid them around his neck, stepping forward until soft curves pressed against hard muscle.

With a gentle tug, she encouraged him to kiss her. It was a mind-numbing interlude. She only made vague notice of the fact that Jesse had unzipped her skirt.

The kiss ended, but the seduction did not. His lips and hands continued their enchantment of her body as Jesse removed her shoes and the rest of her clothing. When he'd finished, he stood back and looked.

Her first instinct was to try to cover as much as she could, but when she saw how moved Jesse was by what he was looking at, she kept her hands at her sides. The expression on his face and the impressive bulge fighting against the denim of his jeans sent a surge of feminine power through her.

"Where are you hiding the third tattoo?" he asked.

Turning slowly, she lifted her hair to expose the red Valentine heart next to her shoulder blade. She let her hair fall, but before she could turn around Jesse came up tightly behind her, one arm around her waist, the other he trailed across her breasts, then downward to slip between her thighs.

Holly gasped, startled by the intensity of the physical sensations he was creating. He started to increase the intimacy of his touch.

In a voice she barely recognized as her own, she said, "Jesse, I, um, please be gentle."

"Let's save gentle for next time. We've both waited too long for this."

She turned in his arms, wedged her hands onto his hair-roughened chest. "I *have* waited a long time. That's why I need you to be gentle."

The fierce desire in his eyes was so strong, Holly wasn't sure he was even beginning to understand what she was trying to say.

His eyes narrowed. "When was the last time you made love?"

"There isn't a last time. This will be my first."

He immediately stepped away, his expression somewhere between disbelief and alarm. "You've never done this before?"

"Not in this lifetime." She fought the urge to grab her clothes to hide behind or make a dash for the bed.

"But... the way you dress."

The same old prejudices. "Because I choose to wear provocative clothing automatically means that I sleep around?"

"There's also the way you kiss."

"I kiss you the way you kiss me."

He turned his back to her, swearing under his breath. With one hand he rubbed the back of his neck.

"You know, you're a hypocrite, Jess. You criticize the women who want you for your Yankee Hunk image, but you're as bad as they are. You were chasing my hot, biker-chick image. Now the image is shattered, you don't want me anymore."

She felt the muscles of her throat tighten. No way was she going to let him see her cry.

Jesse stood staring at the bathroom door. The noise of its slamming echoed in the room.

He was staring at the door, but his eyes were still seeing the last glimpse of Holly disappearing from sight—gloriously naked, her long hair swinging across her back, the smooth flare of womanly hips, and those legs....

He groaned.

A virgin!

He didn't want to believe it. But he knew Holly wouldn't lie. Especially not when he was only a pair of blue jeans away from being able to discover the truth.

Her words about how he was as bad as the women who were chasing him had struck home. Struck home and stuck. He *had* made assumptions about her and the level of her sexual experience by the way she looked and the way she dressed.

But she'd been dead wrong when she said he didn't want her anymore. Lord help him, but he wanted her more than ever!

She might not have had sex before, but she was a sensual, sexy woman who was ready and willing. *She* had asked him to make love.

Why?

Why after waiting this long, had she decided to surrender herself to *him*?

Holly stood in the center of the sumptuous bathroom and wiped at the tears on her cheeks. She kept listening for the sound of the bedroom door into the hallway to open, indicating that Jesse was leaving, but she heard only silence.

What had she done to deserve this? All she'd tried to do was help out a guy in need and earn a little extra cash—well, all right, a lot of cash—but was it enough to make up for the shock therapy her hormones were taking?

If she was going to be stuck naked in the bathroom, she might as well make the most of it. While the sunken tub filled with water, she pinned her hair into a bun. She decided to pass on the Jacuzzi, simply climbing into the warm water. Leaning her head against an indentation in the marble, she lay back and tried to relax.

Yeah, right. Relax!

How, when every nerve ending in her body screamed out in protest at being stimulated to the brink and then left high and dry?

Why hadn't she kept quiet about being a virgin? It would all be over by now if she had. She and Jesse would be lovers by now.

She heard the doorknob turning. *Darn,* why hadn't she locked it?

"Holly?"

She kept her eyes closed. "Yes."

"I wanted to let you know that you're wrong. I *do* still want you."

Opening her eyes, she turned her head. He was standing a few feet away, his arms folded across his still bare chest. "Actions speak louder than words, sweetcheeks."

"Are you sure?"

Was she? "Yes."

Holly watched him run his hands through his hair. He seemed so strong, so self-assured. But underneath she could sense a battle going on. He'd admitted that he wanted her, but he seemed hesitant about following through.

He slipped his hands into the pockets of his jeans. "Why now? Why me?"

"Because of the way I feel when you kiss me." *Because my body is sensing and responding to the powerful need in yours.*

"What do you feel?"

"I feel like I want more. Like kisses aren't enough."

"You've never felt that before?"

She shook her head. "No."

"You're not doing this so you can sell your story to the tabloids?"

She bit her tongue, knowing he'd probably met women who would do just that. "I have too much respect for myself than to want my sex life broadcast throughout the free world. And I have too much respect for you."

He was quiet for a moment, then spoke. "I'll do what I can, but the first time isn't usually the best for a woman."

"I know what to expect. Between friends, movies and the media, I know quite a bit about sex. I'm a virgin, but I'm not naive."

Her tattoos hadn't been painless, either, but she'd tolerated the pain to get the finished product and she was willing to accept the pain of giving up her virginity to experience being one with Jesse.

To fully savor the experience of being his fiancée—if only for a short time.

He nodded. "All right."

The click of the foil packet he dropped on the tile next to the tub drew her attention. A sharp edge of reality punctured the gossamer of the sensual fantasy she'd let the moonlight and Jesse's kisses wrap her in.

She was gripped by a sense of panic. What in heaven's name was she getting herself into? And why?

The popping sound of a snap opening and the drag of a zipper drew her gaze elsewhere, and she knew the answer to both her questions.

Eight

Holly watched as Jesse took off his boots, then slid out of his jeans and briefs. There was no doubt that he wanted her. And, oh, how she wanted him. The first time she'd seen him in the tattoo parlor, she'd thought he was a major hunk.

Was he ever!

Her gaze wandered to the mirror behind him and the breathtaking view it gave her of his sleek, tight buns.

"Should I get out?"

"No, I'm coming in. Scoot forward." Jesse got in behind her. He wrapped his arms around her waist, pulling her against his warmth. She felt him placing soft, openmouthed kisses along the sides and back of her neck as he roamed his hands slowly over her.

"You know, we can take care of the immediate problem without actually making love."

"I—" Her words were cut off when he slipped one of his hands between her legs. A shiver raced through her.

He murmured words of encouragement between the continuing shower of kisses. One hand he trailed across her—lingering, caressing.

While with the other he kept going further and further with his tantalizing foray—small circular caresses, sleek strokes and finally the gentle, shallow probing that left her gasping for breath and feeling like she might explode into a thousand pieces.

Tilting her head, she looked over her shoulder. "Jess." It was a whispered plea.

He lowered his lips onto hers and kissed her. Holly kissed him back. He accelerated the onslaught on her senses until she quivered on the brink—not knowing whether she wanted to beg him to stop, or beg him never to stop.

"Come on, Holly. That's it. Let go, baby. Just let go."

Leaning her head against his shoulder, arching her back and crying out his name, she complied. Nothing existed for her in those long moments of ecstasy except Jesse—the solidness of his body against hers, the taste of his kisses, the sound of his voice, the magic of his hands.

As she slowly floated to reality, one of the first things she was aware of was Jesse's arousal, hard, hot and pressing against her.

The moment had arrived and the choice was hers. Did she return the favor he'd granted, or did they make love? Turning in his arms, she met his gaze.

He smiled and placed a soft kiss on her love-swollen lips. "You are one beautiful, sexy lady."

She felt the warm rush of blood to her cheeks. "I, um, I don't know what to say."

"Did you like it?"

"Oh-hh, yes." She reached her arms around his neck. "Can we make love now?"

"Are you sure? We're not going to be able to undo this once it's done."

"I know."

"And I don't want you to feel pressured."

She wiggled against him. "Pressured?"

He said something under his breath that she couldn't decipher. Before she had time to ask him to repeat it, he had shifted her around until she straddled him. He reached over and retrieved the foil packet, then while his kiss distracted her and his hands rekindled the desire he'd momentarily quenched, he leaned forward and kept leaning until she was underneath him.

He was over her, then he was in her. . . .

At her quick intake of breath, he stilled and moved his lips from hers. "Are you all right?"

Was she?

The sharp pain was fading, leaving her with a tight feeling of fullness. Jesse. She was making love with Jesse. She smiled. "I'm fine. How are you?"

He chuckled. "About to explode."

"I thought that was the whole idea."

"Eventually, but we don't want it to be over before it's begun."

He shifted his hips and began a slow, sensual rhythm that had Holly gasping. In no time she felt ready to explode, too. As she had before, she relinquished command of her body to the mastery of his.

His movements took on an urgent, driven edge, as though he was no longer in complete control, either. Holly wrapped her arms and legs more tightly around him.

With no warning, ecstasy grabbed hold of her again. Deep within her, Jesse shared it more fully this time and took his own release in the aftershocks of hers.

Gently he reversed their positions until she was laying over him. He reached out and turned on the water jets. The heated water bubbled around them. Holly rested her head against his shoulder and relaxed against him. He held her close, caressing her back.

She had no regrets. She was glad Jesse had been her first. It was impossible to imagine that she would ever have found another lover to handle her initiation with such kindness and consideration. Yes, Jesse had been kind and considerate.

Kind and considerate.

The words repeated over and over, until she connected them to the memory she'd been searching for. Kind, considerate, established and settled—the four requirements she'd promised herself in a husband.

She sat up quickly.

"Holly, are you okay?"

She looked into his worried eyes and forced her mind away from its troubling thoughts. It was silly to fret about Jesse matching her requirements for a husband. Not only did he match her requirements, but her mother's as well—rich and successful.

Was she falling into the trap she'd been so adamant about avoiding? No, she hadn't been chasing him, he'd come to her and this arrangement was only for a week.

He'd said absolutely nothing about the future, not even whether they would ever see each other after the week was over.

Just because she'd slept with a man didn't mean she was starting to become like her mother. She still had her own dreams, her own career plans. Making love with Jesse didn't change that...even if they did happen to see each other after this week, she didn't have to surrender her plan.

She smiled. "I'm fine. Wonderful, in fact."

"You can say that again."

"You were wonderful, too." She playfully trailed her fingers across his chest. "And I can honestly say you're the best lover I've ever had."

Jesse rolled his eyes. "Come on, let's go to bed." He shifted her off him and set her on the edge of the tub.

"Does that mean I don't have to sleep on the couch?"

Holly had never been in bed with a man before. It would be easy to get used to—lying in the dark, held securely in strong male arms, listening to Jesse's rhythmic breathing, feeling the rise and fall of his chest.

She wondered again at the strange things she felt with him. Could she be falling in love? Or was she falling in lust? Or was she merely reacting to the role she was playacting? Or overreacting to it?

It was heady stuff having people think they were a couple. What was it Joanna had said? That she must be a special lady to have gotten Jesse to commit.

She did feel special in a way she'd never experienced before. Jesse made her feel special.

Early the next morning he woke her with kisses and, after being assured she was only a little sore, he made love to her. Being in a king-size bed rather than a tub of water, gave them a great deal more freedom to explore and be explored.

By the time he aligned their bodies for joining, Holly could barely remember her name. She moved her hips upward to meet him, welcoming him into her. Together they spiraled in a whirlpool of ecstasy.

Giving pleasure, receiving pleasure—until they reached the ultimate shared satisfaction.

Jesse lifted his weight onto his elbows. "Well, it wasn't just my imagination."

"You thought it might be?"

"I couldn't believe it had really been so perfect."

If Jesse, who had much more experience with these things than she did, was surprised by the intensity of their lovemaking, no wonder she was dazed by it. Slowly, he moved until he lay next to her.

Holly turned her head on the pillow and looked at him. "Guess I wasn't as immune to your charms as you thought I was."

He ran one finger lazily along the sensitive skin of her inner arm. "We've spent time together, gotten to know each other. You didn't fawn all over me from the very beginning."

"The fawning really bothers you, doesn't it?"

"Yes. There's more to me than the way I look."

"You want a woman to be immune to your charms? It's real easy. Threaten her with a lawsuit." He stopped his idle stroking of her arm. "And before you ask, no, I did *not* go to bed with you so you wouldn't press charges."

Jesse rolled onto his side and propped himself on his elbow. "I wasn't going to suggest anything of the sort."

"Then why do you have that guilty look on your face?"

"Because there isn't going to be a lawsuit."

She sat up. "No lawsuit?"

"Chad was perfectly happy to accept your father's promise that the design wouldn't be used again."

She didn't want to believe it. "You've known all along? But you let me think..." He'd let her think a lawsuit was still a possibility, that her actions might have put her father's business in jeopardy.

"I thought it might help persuade you to accept my offer."

"It did." She slid to the end of the bed, grabbed a discarded towel from the night before and wrapped it around herself. "Do you think not telling me there was no danger of a lawsuit was a fair thing to do?"

"Probably not."

"Definitely not!"

Jesse got off the bed, walked to the closet and started dressing. "Was that the only reason you agreed to come here with me?"

"No."

"Then don't make a big deal out of it."

Don't make a big deal out of it! That was easy for him to say.

"Did you hope I would offer to sleep with you to stop you from pressing charges?"

His hands stilled in their task of buttoning his shirt. "What kind of sleazy character do you think I am?"

"That's what I'm trying to figure out."

The phone rang. Since she was closest, Holly picked it up.

"Hi, Holly. It's Joanna. Is Jesse ready? He promised to help me pick out a wedding gift for Doug."

"He's right here, Joanna." She tossed the receiver onto the bed and walked away, going to the closet to get her clothes.

"Hi, JoJo," she heard Jesse say. There was a pause and then he said, "We'll be right down."

It took every ounce of control and acting ability Holly had to play the loving fiancée when she was so angry at Jesse. She hid her fuming behind a bright smile and reminded herself there were only a few more days of this to get through.

And a few more nights....

But she didn't want to think about those.

The shopping trip went smoothly. Joanna bought Doug a new leather briefcase and made arrangements for it to be monogrammed and delivered.

The three of them arrived at the house just as the UPS truck was pulling out of the driveway.

"Anyone up for helping me open presents?"

"You're going to open them now?" Holly asked.

"Mother insists the gifts be opened and displayed as they arrive."

If she helped Joanna, it would postpone her having to be alone with Jesse, so Holly volunteered.

She suspected he was still angry about the remark she'd made. That was fine with her, she was still an-

gry that he'd known all along there was no lawsuit in
the works but had let her think otherwise.

And the ironic thing was, that even without the
threatened legal action, she probably would have
made the trip with him anyway—the money was
generous, the chance to get the inside story on any
potential clothing line was important, but what had
carried the most weight were the stories she'd read in
the papers and magazines about a young man who'd
had the courage to stand up to his family and say no
to the easy road.

A few of the bridesmaids also helped with the
gifts. Mrs. Tyler came in as they were finishing and
suggested Joanna show Holly the stables. Since Mrs.
Tyler had ignored her most of the week, Holly suspected it wasn't just an impromptu idea, that there
was some reason behind it.

There were two separate stables on the premises.
Joanna explained that one was for the horses they
rode and used recreationally, while the other was for
the polo ponies and breeding stock.

Joanna stopped in front of one of the stalls. She
looked at her feet, then at Holly. "I hesitate to bring
this up, and if I hadn't promised Mother, I probably
wouldn't mention it at all. Please don't take this
personally, but she's worried about what you're
planning to wear to the wedding."

Holly thought about the outfit hanging in the
closet upstairs. Flashy and sexy, not something most
would consider appropriate for an afternoon wed-

ding. It was just the sort of outfit Jesse's mother was afraid she'd show up in.

But this wasn't Jesse's mother's wedding. It was Joanna's. She was sure once she reminded Jesse of this, he would agree that she should leave off the masquerade for the wedding itself. After all, it was his parents he'd wanted to shake up, not Joanna.

"You can assure your mother that her future daughter-in-law will be dressed for the occasion."

Now all she had to do was convince Jesse.

She found him in their room, lounging on the couch with a laptop computer. The screen held an assortment of numbers and strange symbols.

"Your Christmas list?" she said, hoping that by lightening the mood the argument from this morning would be forgotten.

He glanced at her, then looked down and hit a few keys. "I'm running some test results for a new carburetor system."

She sat on the chair closest to him. "I've been thinking, maybe I should wear something a bit more conservative to the wedding."

He continued pressing keys. "We had an agreement."

"So, dock my pay by the percentage of an evening."

He looked at her, his expression cool.

Holly continued. "Listen, at a wedding the bride is supposed to be the one holding center stage."

"I've been to plenty of weddings where some of the female guests dressed to make sure they got more than their share of attention."

"Me, too. And there may be some at Joanna's, but I'm not going to be one of them."

He looked at his watch, pushed a few more keys, then shut off the laptop. "I don't have time to argue with you. Alex, Rorke and I have a conference call scheduled."

She had hoped he would see her point and offer to take her shopping for something new to wear to the wedding. By the time they got back to their discussion and she was able to convince him to take her, there wouldn't be much time left before he had to get ready for the evening's bachelor party.

She would have to get herself there. From downstairs she could call a taxi, or maybe Joanna would let her borrow her car. As she started for the door, she caught sight of Jesse's keys on the dresser. If she asked, he would probably say no, but a conference call with his partners meant business, so he would be busy for a while. She might even be able to get back before he knew she'd gone.

She had no trouble finding the Yankee in the garage behind the house. It shared one of the spaces with Joanna's car. Carefully, she rolled it out onto the driveway. For its size, it was lighter than she'd expected. Heavier than hers, but not more than she thought she could handle safely. She straddled the bike. It took her a few minutes to find the keyhole, but the other controls were placed as they were on hers.

She pushed the starter and the engine roared to life. There was an intoxicating power rush as she set off down the driveway. Her legs were wrapped around Jesse's bike as not so long ago they'd been wrapped around the man himself. Would she ever have the opportunity to do that again?

There was the lawsuit argument and now the dress issue between them. Although, once he'd thought about it, she was sure he would see her side of the dress thing. She hoped.

The day of the bridesmaid's luncheon she'd noticed a consignment shop in the shopping center near the restaurant. She headed that way.

"I think that about covers it," Alex Dalton said. "Unless either of you has something to add."

"Not me," Rorke said.

"Me, either," Jesse said.

"How's Callie doing?" Alex asked.

"She's getting impatient. The nursery's ready. All that's missing is a baby."

It seemed like yesterday that Rorke had told them Callie was expecting. Hell, it seemed like yesterday that the three of them had been single. Jesse felt a stab of nostalgic regret for those days when after a long day of work they'd hit a party together. Although they rarely left together, none of them left alone.

"And how are things going with the wedding preparations, Jesse?"

"All right, but I'm looking forward to getting back to work." *Coward, you just want to get away from Holly.* The sex had been incredible, mind-blowing, but their argument this morning and the one this afternoon worried him. Couples fought. Relationships in the throes of development needed fine tuning. He and Holly were not a couple, they were not building a relationship, so they shouldn't be fighting.

Rorke laughed. "Back to work? You're starting to have a one-track mind."

"You told me you were going to have a good time down there. What happened?" Alex asked.

"Hey, you two, lighten up." His tone sounded more abrupt than he'd meant it to.

There was silence on both lines for a moment, then Rorke said, "Dalton, do you see a pattern here? Obsession with work, inability to take a little friendly teasing, barking at your friends..."

Alex gave a low whistle. "What's her name, Jesse?"

"I don't have the slightest idea what you're talking about." *Man, he wished that were true.*

"He's got it bad," Rorke said.

"I think you're right," Alex said. "Details, Jesse, give us details."

Someone began to whistle "The Wedding March."

"Don't hold your breath, guys."

They were both laughing when he hung up the phone.

What was it with married guys, anyway? They always seemed to want everyone else to tie the knot, too. Was it a case of misery loves company?

But neither Rorke nor Alex was miserable. In fact, they were both disgustingly happy.

He thought about getting his laptop out again, but decided maybe he should talk to Holly—settle their differences. He had to hand it to her, she'd handled their shopping trip with Joanna without giving any sign of the argument they'd been having. He thought he'd handled himself quite well, too.

His plans for a talk were hindered by the fact that he couldn't find Holly anywhere.

Several hours after leaving the Tyler house, Holly put the Yankee where she'd found it, gathered her purchases from the saddlebags and headed for the house.

Jesse met her in the middle of the driveway. "What in the hell were you thinking?"

Nine

Holly placed her free hand on her hip. "I wanted to do some shopping and you were busy."

"You could have borrowed one of the cars, or my parents' limo."

"I prefer motorcycles and I've been riding for years."

Jesse ran one hand through his hair. His mouth was pressed together in a thin line. It looked as though he was struggling not to lose his temper. "My bike is heavier and has a more powerful engine than yours."

"And it handles like a dream. I had a great cruise, Jess. Don't ruin it for me." She started to walk past him toward the house.

He reached one arm across her path. "I don't want you on that bike again, except as a passenger."

She knew some bikers were ultrapossessive of their bikes, maybe Jesse was one of them. "I didn't hurt your bike."

"I'm not worried about the bike. The bike can be replaced. But what if something had happened to you?"

"I've got insurance and I'd venture to guess you do, too."

"And how do you think your father would feel if I showed up at his shop with the news you'd been hurt in a motorcycle accident?"

"Look, my dad rides, too, and he knows motorcycles are dangerous. I've taken motorcycle safety courses, both beginning and advanced. And I wouldn't have borrowed your bike if I hadn't been totally confident in my ability to handle it." Over his shoulder, she caught sight of several horses with riders coming across the lawn in their general direction. "Maybe we should continue this argument somewhere less public."

He glanced behind him, then turned, putting his arm around her waist. "Shall we go in, then?"

To keep up appearances, she stayed within the curve of his arm and let him escort her to their room.

Holly set Jesse's keys on the dresser as she walked past on her way to the closet. She hung up her new outfit. It wasn't likely that she'd heard the last of Jesse's objections on the subject of what she was wearing to the wedding, but at the moment he seemed more concerned about her motorcycle ride.

When she turned around, Jesse was standing across the room, looking out the window. Memories of how gentle he'd been with her last night and what an incredible lover he was flooded her senses.

Suddenly she wanted nothing more than to run across the room and throw herself into his arms. The man was pure temptation... temptation in motorcycle boots.

If she thought he would be receptive, she would be across the room in a heartbeat. But the stiff line of his back and the tight line of his shoulders told her he was still angry.

"I'm sorry I borrowed your bike, Jesse."

He turned, a skeptical look on his face. "Really?"

"Well, I'm sorry I got *caught* borrowing your bike."

The briefest trace of a smile played at the corners of his mouth. "That one I believe."

"It really was a great ride. I've never driven a Yankee before. For such a big bike it corners easily. I was very impressed."

"Resorting to flattery?"

She wrinkled her nose at him. "So, what time is the bachelor party?"

"Trying to get rid of me?"

"Just wondering if we would be going downstairs for dinner before you left. I'll need to shower and change if we are."

He rubbed one hand across the back of his neck. "Why don't we have something sent up?"

"All right," she agreed, but then perversely wondered why he wanted to stay upstairs.

Did he want the evening off from pretending to be in love with her? Was he tired of the charade? She should be grateful for the break.

You will be grateful, Holly. Maybe if she repeated it enough times.

"Are you hungry now?" he asked.

"Not much."

"In an hour, then?"

"Sure."

They were polite strangers. It was hard to believe that less than twelve hours ago they'd been curled up together in the bed, and that the bedding, which now lay so smoothly, had once been a tangled mess. "I guess I'll shower anyway. That is, unless you'd like to use the bathroom first."

"You go ahead. I'll wait."

Jesse lay on the couch, one forearm covering his eyes, and listened to the water running in the shower. It was easy for him to visualize Holly standing naked in the spacious shower stall. There was a persistent ache in a part of his anatomy that was doing its best to encourage him to shed his clothing and join her.

He was giving it serious consideration, but several things were bothering him. First was the sense of panic that had seized him when he'd discovered his bike was missing and he'd instantly suspected Holly was on it. Second was the overwhelming gratitude he'd felt when she'd ridden up the driveway.

Both reactions had been extreme and intense. Much more so than they should have been given the circumstances.

Sure it would have been awkward contacting Red Bryant if anything had happened to her, but as she'd pointed out, as a rider her father knew the dangers involved.

Maybe it was Rorke and Alex's teasing that had knocked his emotions out of alignment. Or maybe it was some strange reaction to the recent end of his run of celibacy.

Whatever... it was probably best not to dwell on it.

He swung his legs to the side and stood. He crossed the room to the bathroom door as he had last night. But this time the door was locked.

Holly spent the evening working in her sketchbook. It did wonders to soothe her frazzled nerves. From the time she'd come out of the shower until Jesse had finally left for the bachelor party, they'd continued in the same stiff, polite manner they'd fallen into after their fight in the driveway.

The more she moved her pencil across the paper, the calmer she got. She was feeling almost normal when Jesse's cellular phone rang. She wasn't sure whether she should answer it or not. There was a slim chance it was Jesse calling her.

Right! They were barely speaking to each other, and he's going to call her to chat in the middle of a bachelor party.

She decided to answer anyway, in case it was an important call. It was a woman with a Southern accent asking for Jesse.

"I'm afraid he's not here at the moment."

"Darn!"

"Would you like to leave a message?"

"Is this Joanna?"

"No. I'm Holly, a friend of Jesse's. Why don't you give me your name and number and I'll have him call you back."

"He doesn't need to call me back. Just tell him Genie called and that Rorke asked me to pass on the news that it's a boy."

Holly tore a sheet from her sketchbook and jotted down the information. The name Genie didn't sound familiar, but she was pretty sure Rorke was one of Jesse's partners. "I'll be sure Jesse gets the message."

* * *

Jesse yawned as he walked through the front door of his parents' house. He would have left the party long before he did, but he'd promised Joanna he would be sure Douglas got home safely.

He found Joanna in the den watching a movie with a group of friends. He noticed Holly wasn't with them.

After assuring his sister that he'd accomplished his mission, he headed for the stairs.

"Hello, Jesse. How was the party?"

Jesse turned to see Darlene standing in the living room doorway. "It was a typical bachelor party."

She tilted her head, then pointed up. "Mistletoe, Jesse."

"Have you taken up botany?"

Her bottom lip slid forward in a flirty pout. "You don't have to be a botanist to know that standing under the mistletoe means you're supposed to get a kiss."

"I'm engaged, Darlene."

"Your fiancée has been upstairs all evening. I'm sure she's fast asleep. Come to my room for a few hours, she'll never know."

"I'll know."

Slowly, Darlene took a few sliding steps until she stood about a foot away from him.

He looked to where her plunging neckline left little to the imagination. Mentally he shoved the fabric a few inches to the side and waited for his heartbeat to quicken and the familiar rush of blood to his groin to begin.

He waited. But he felt nothing.

Absolutely nothing!

It was several hours after Holly had taken the phone call that Jesse returned. He stood, just inside the doorway, and looked at her. Holly felt the urge to run to him again. Instead she picked up the paper with the message on it.

"You had a phone call."

He walked over, took the message from her, then went and sat on the end of the bed.

"A boy. It's a boy." There was a touch of wonder in his voice.

"That's what she said. That her name was Genie and Rorke said to tell you it was a boy."

"Genie is my partner Alex's wife. Rorke is the other partner, and his wife, Callie, just had a baby. A baby boy."

A second generation Yankee Hunk!

Watch out, females of the future.

Holly waited for Jesse to say more, but he continued staring at the paper.

Then he smiled and looked across the room at her. "It's a boy."

"Would it have been so very terrible if it had been a girl?"

Jesse laughed. "No, a girl would have been fine, too. It's just that it didn't seem real before, when it was just a baby... but when it's a boy, or a girl, then it's real... a little person..."

He was so delighted with the news, Holly wondered if he intended having a family in the future. "Do you plan to have children?"

After a moment of silence, he answered. "Yeah, I think I would like kids someday. Someone to take over my share of Yankee."

"What if your children aren't interested in motorcycles?"

"That would make their grandparents happy."

Holly stood and walked across the room to sit next to him. "It might make their grandparents happy, but how would you feel about it?"

"I'd be disappointed. Yankee is so much a part of me, of course I'd want to share that with my children."

"But your children aren't you, Jess. Any more than you were your parents."

"Are you trying to point out, not too subtly by the way, that instead of making my parents angry, my disliking horses disappointed them?"

"Yes. And I think they're a little jealous, too."

Jesse laughed. "Think again, sweetheart. I might have more money than I'll ever need, but it will be a while before I catch up with my parents."

"Maybe, but they never worked for it. The money was there, the houses were there. Don't you think that might bother their egos? They were handed everything. You went out into the world and competed successfully for what you've got. I'll bet they envy you your accomplishments. After all, they're *your* accomplishments."

"Not just mine. Don't forget Alex and Rorke. Rorke built that first bike with me, and Alex is a business wiz."

"That's still different than inheriting everything."

"So, Dr. Bryant, in their disappointment and jealousy, my parents disown me and tell me never to darken their doorstep again."

"Yeah, something like that."

"Great bedtime story."

Holly frowned. "You don't think I'm right?"

"There might be some truth in it, but I don't think it's as cut-and-dried as you make it sound. Nothing ever is."

"I know. Kind of like the question of whether or not you should have told me up front that there wasn't going to be a lawsuit."

"Exactly."

"I'm sorry about this morning, Jess. I know you wouldn't have used the lawsuit to try to seduce me. I was angry and spoke without thinking."

"And I'm sorry I didn't tell you the truth up front."

Impulsively, she reached her arms around his neck and hugged him. She started to move away, but his arms closed around her. Looking deep into his eyes, she let herself sink once again into the magic illusion that they were a couple.

When he kissed her, she kissed him back. When he started to remove her clothing, she did the same to his. Once they were both undressed and standing next to the bed, he took her in his arms again and held her close.

Holly snuggled against him, inhaling the spiciness of his after-shave and absorbing the warmth of his skin. The few quiet moments were the calm before the storm. And the storm hit without warning—powerful and overwhelmingly sensual.

With her hands and mouth she touched and tasted, while Jesse did the same. Leaning forward, he turned his expert attention to her breasts, teasing the peaks into hard nubs and soothing the tight achiness by cupping her in his warm palms.

He sat on the edge of the bed and continued placing kisses along her in a descending path. Holly sucked in her breath as he passed her holly tattoo and slowly continued on. Her hands clutched at his shoulders, clinging to the solid, tangible, warm male whose hands, lips and tongue were propelling her deeper and deeper into the sensual storm.

She tingled where he touched, but the effects spread far afield from the top of her head to the tips of her curling toes.

When her knees no longer seemed able to hold her up, Jesse lay across the bed, pulling her gently until she lay over him. She leaned forward to kiss him, her hair draping around them like a curtain.

He returned the kiss with a thoroughness that left her throbbing with need and desire. When he moved his hands to her hips, she lifted onto her knees. Holding his gaze, she wrapped her legs around him and welcomed him into her.

The throaty rasp he made could have been mistaken for pain, but the heat flaring in his eyes made it clear that what he was feeling was intense pleasure.

So was Holly.

She boldly experimented with movement and tempo—testing the possibilities and zeroing in on what felt best. Her vantage point gave her a chance to watch the play of emotions on Jesse's face. It delivered the same rush of power as being on a long, empty stretch of road and opening the throttle on a motorcycle. There was the rush and reverence for the power beneath you. And there was the pleasure in knowing the power was in your control.

But then her own traitorous body wrestled the control from her, tumbling her over the edge. Jesse tumbled with her, arching up and at the same time spanning his hands across her lower back pressing her even tighter against him.

Holly collapsed on his chest. She closed her eyes and lay listening as the steady beat of his heart gradually slowed to a normal rate. He placed a soft kiss on top of her head.

"Jesse," she said his name somewhere between a whisper and a sigh.

When they'd recovered enough, they turned off the lights and crawled beneath the covers. Wrapped securely in Jesse's arms, Holly drifted off immediately.

Jesse woke with the sun and knew he wouldn't be able to go back to sleep. Holly was sleeping so peacefully, he didn't want to disturb her, although he considered kissing her awake to make love to her again. Instead he got up, dressed, and strolled to the stables. He'd been avoiding them since he'd arrived.

The familiar scent of hay and horses reached him even before he entered the open double doors. Memories came flooding back.

He'd taken riding lessons as a young boy. He'd done well enough, he supposed, but even then he'd had a preference for the gardener's riding mower over his pony.

He walked through the stable, stopping to look into some of the stalls along the way. A brass nameplate hung above each, identifying the occupant. Jesse remembered taking this same walk with his father. His father had greeted each horse by name, then had started quizzing Jesse, expecting "his son" to take the same interest.

Fathers and sons....

Rorke had a son.... Someday he might have a child.

He thought about Holly's question of what he would do if his children didn't like motorcycles. It would definitely be a disappointment. His third of Yankee was quite an empire already and the future prospects were good. He liked the idea of passing it to his heirs. It would be nice if future generations of Tylers, Daltons and O'Neils continued to run Yankee together.

Had his parents felt this way about the Tyler holdings?

Had it been disappointment that had driven their negative reaction to his fascination with man-made horsepower rather than the real thing?

Despite any disappointment, he still couldn't imagine that he would disown his own children because they didn't like motorcycles. He hoped he would be open-minded enough to allow his kids to find their own happiness and not try to make them clones of himself. He hoped he would have the strength to support them in their own choices.

Of course all this contemplation on having children was totally theoretical. Without a special someone in his life, he wasn't likely to have the opportunity to be a parent.

He wondered how Holly felt about kids.

What in heaven's name was he thinking?

The sound of horse hooves approaching caught his attention. He turned and saw Joanna leading a horse into the stable.

"You're up early, JoJo."

"So are you. I wish you'd been here half an hour ago, I would have taken you riding with me."

"Or I might have stuck you on the back of my bike and taken you for a ride."

Joanna shrugged. "Either way I would have gotten to breathe the fresh morning air and feel the wind in my face. But with the horse I didn't have to listen to an engine making all that racket."

"I love the sound of 'all that racket.' Besides, a running horse isn't very quiet."

Joanna opened the door to one of the stalls. A groom appeared as if by magic and took the reins from her. She walked to Jesse and linked her arm with his. "Actually, today I wouldn't have minded the racket. I just needed to get away. I can't wait until the wedding is over."

"Is it really that bad?"

"At times. Mother is making such a production of this whole thing that sometimes I lose track of what it's all really about. I get wrapped up in the details and forget about loving Douglas and the fact that the reason for the wedding is so we can pledge the rest of our lives to each other." Her eyes glittered with tears. "With all the particulars it's easy to lose track of the love that brought us together in the first place. I miss the happy moments of being together without having to discuss this or that and get back to Mother with the decision."

Happy moments of being together. Something twisted inside him.

"Was it the happy moments that let you know you were in love with Douglas?"

"Of course. Isn't that how you knew you were in love with Holly?"

Ten

The activity level in the house on the final day before the wedding was hectic. All of the downstairs rooms and hallways were decked out for the wedding or Christmas or a combination of the two. The regular staff and the wedding consultant's team were busily going about their business. Holly did her best to stay out of the way.

There was no sign of Jesse.

It had surprised her to waken to find herself alone. She'd been looking forward to waking in Jesse's arms as she had the morning before, hoping the peace and contentment would last today as it hadn't yesterday.

Holly recognized most of the people in the dining room from the other night, but there were also some new arrivals. She had a small breakfast, then took a cup of coffee and sat on the patio.

Preparations for tomorrow's festivities were also taking place on the lawn, along with a group of children playing croquet. She watched as she sipped her coffee. Her cup was almost empty when she spotted Jesse and Joanna heading across the lawn from the direction of the stables. She stood as they came closer.

Jesse greeted her with a brief, good-morning kiss. She wished she knew if the kiss was for Holly the pretend fiancée or for Holly the woman he'd made love to last night. Regardless of who it was for, it sent her heartbeat racing.

Joanna and Holly exchanged greetings.

"I was wondering where you were," Holly said to Jesse.

"I went for a walk."

Was he regretting what had happened between them last night? His expression gave nothing away.

Mrs. Tyler came bustling onto the patio. "There you are, Joanna. I need you in the library immediately. And, Jesse, I can't remember if I mentioned it or not, but tomorrow evening, after the reception, we'll be having a Christmas party for the family. You and Ms. Bryant are welcome to attend." She didn't give Jesse time to respond before turning and retracing her steps.

"Duty calls," Joanna said. She gave Jesse and Holly each a quick hug, then hurried after her mother.

Jesse tucked his hands into the pockets of his blue jeans. "Would you like to go to the Christmas party?"

"It's up to you. We can go if you'd like."

He was quiet for a moment. "I think I'd like to."

"All right then." Holly was intrigued by Jesse's decision. She would be willing to bet that if the invitation to the Christmas party had been issued when they'd first arrived, he would have turned it down flat. It seemed that, despite himself, there was a tentative bridge forming between Jesse and his parents. "What's on the agenda for today?"

"This evening is the rehearsal and the rehearsal dinner. You can have the rest of the day free if you'd like."

At some point she was going to have to bring up the question of her clothes for the wedding again. But it would be better if they were alone when she did. "What are you going to do?"

"First, I think I'll head upstairs and order flowers for Callie and the new baby."

Did he want her to go with him? "That's a nice idea. I'm sure she'll appreciate them."

"I don't know. Rorke may already have filled her room with flowers."

"What about a bouquet of balloons, then, or a stuffed teddy bear, or maybe a gift basket with an assortment of baby things?"

"You've done this type of thing before?"

"You haven't?"

"My secretary takes care of it, but she's got the week off, too. So I figured I'd handle it myself."

"There's a shop I use in Daytona Beach that does gift baskets and stuffed animals. They ship all over the country and have overnight service available. I think I have their card upstairs in my purse."

Once upstairs, Jesse placed the order and Holly went to brush her teeth. When she walked into the bedroom, she found Jesse standing by the couch. He was holding the sketchbook she'd abandoned on the coffee table last night when he'd returned.

"I take it this is yours?"

"Yes."

"A hobby?"

"No, fashion design is what I'm studying in school."

"These sketches are very good."

"Thank you."

"There has been some discussion of adding a clothing line at Yankee."

Something in the stiffness of his stance bothered her. It crossed her mind to act surprised, to pretend this was the first she knew of it. "I'd heard there was the possibility."

"Is that what last night's apology and cuddling up was for?"

"No. I'll admit it was part of the reason I accepted your offer in the first place, but it has nothing whatsoever to do with anything that has gone on here. Not the apologies . . . not the sex."

He dropped the sketchbook onto the couch. "Then what was last night about?"

Holly wanted to scream with frustration. Instead she took a deep breath and counted to ten before answering. "Stop looking for ulterior motives from me, Jesse."

"That's your answer?"

"I don't owe you any explanations."

"Because you don't want to admit that you were trying to get into my good graces to get a shot at a job?"

A whole string of colorful oaths that she'd heard over the years in the tattoo parlor were on the tip of her tongue.

If I weren't a lady, I'd tell you a thing or two, buster!

"I apologized because I was sorry. I made love with you because when you're not acting like a Neanderthal you're a really nice guy!"

He reached into his back pocket and took out his wallet. He removed a business card and held it out to her. "The idea is being considered, but I'm not personally involved in the project, so I can't promise you anything. But send some of your work to Alex Dalton. I'll tell him to watch for it."

She took the card, carefully avoiding any contact with Jesse's fingers. Was it only last night that she'd allowed the same fingers to roam over her body? Now she couldn't even bring herself to let them touch her hand.

But if she touched him, she would want more...she would want to make love with him. Her body ached for it, but then, what wild accusations would he come up with for her behavior if she did?

She'd given herself to him for the sheer joy of being with him, and it hurt knowing that he didn't accept her gift in the same way she offered it.

"Thank you," she said.

"So, the week wasn't a total waste, after all. You got what you came for, a shot at a job."

The accusing tone in his voice infuriated her. "I told you it was one of the things I considered when trying to decide to come this week. But you seem to have forgotten that *you* were the one who asked me here, not the other way around. The whole thing was your idea, and you're the one who came to me with it. I agreed to help you." She walked to the dresser and slipped the business card into her purse. "Now, if you'll excuse me, I think I'll take your offer of an afternoon off."

One by one Jesse sunk ball after ball into the pockets of his father's pool table. The muted sounds of the game soothed his raw nerves.

He'd been on edge since last night when Darlene's attempts to lure him to her bed had failed to create even the slightest stir to his libido. His time with Holly had put to rest any fears of problems with the equipment, but had left him with even more questions.

Their lovemaking had been totally satisfying physically. Emotionally it had created a moment that had come to his mind instantly the minute Joanna had mentioned happy moments of being alone together. The look on his sister's face when she'd said it had prompted him to ask her about falling in love. He'd needed to ask the question, but at the same time he'd been afraid of the answer. Her words had lived up to his worst fear.

He couldn't be falling in love with Holly....

It was obvious she wasn't in love with him.

A woman in love wouldn't have accused him of acting like a Neanderthal. Except, if he was honest, he supposed he had been acting like a Neanderthal.

Holly hadn't sought him out with her drawings, he'd gone to her with his idea for a mock engagement. Then he thought about the rest of what she'd said, that he was "a really nice guy."

Nice.

He wasn't sure how to take that. Most women used the description "nice" when they couldn't think of anything better to say about a guy. But coming from Holly, straightforward Holly, he suspected she'd meant it as a high compliment.

Even so, it wasn't likely to be the way she would describe someone who'd swept her off her feet.

Ah, hell...what difference did it make? It was probably his ego kicking up dust. Even though he didn't like it, he was used to women throwing themselves at him. Perhaps he'd grown so accustomed to it that when it didn't happen it knocked him off-balance.

Only the cue ball was left on the table. He thought about racking them up again, but decided against it. If he and Holly were staying for the Christmas party, he should do something about presents.

Holly longed to "borrow" Jesse's bike again. Riding always had a calming effect on her. At the moment she needed calming. But she knew any benefits she would get from the ride would be destroyed if Jesse found out.

Instead of heading for the garage, she wandered to the stables. A group was getting ready to head out for a ride. On a whim, Holly joined them. By the time they got back, the wedding rehearsal was already under way on the back lawn.

Holly raced upstairs for a quick shower and to change for the rehearsal dinner. The dinner was going to be at the country club, so she assumed it would be a dressy affair. It didn't take long for her to decide to wear the dress she'd originally brought for the wedding—a seductive, red-sequined little number with a heart-shaped neckline. The dress almost reached her knees, but the side slit eliminated any chance of it being considered demure.

Once dressed, she went outside and watched the remainder of the rehearsal. Jesse joined her as soon as his part was finished and kept her by his side the rest of the evening, playing the part of devoted fiancé to the hilt. They shared a limo to and from the dinner with Joanna and Douglas, so Holly and Jesse weren't alone until they returned to their room late in the evening.

"Well, tomorrow's the big day," Holly said.

"Yes. The week's almost over."

Holly wondered whether their paths would ever cross again once their time here was done. Surely they could get together and do lunch, or catch a movie. She tried to imagine it happening, tried to imagine having a casual relationship with this man she'd been intimate with. Her usually vivid imagination was coming up blank.

"About tomorrow, Jess. I meant what I said about wearing something more conservative."

"I thought I made myself clear the other day when I told you that would be a breach of our original agreement."

"I thought maybe since you've had time to think about it you might have changed your mind."

"No, I haven't."

"Jesse, I like your sister."

"And I love my sister, but what does that have to do with this?"

"A wedding is serious business. I'm not going to risk doing anything that might upset your sister. Tomorrow is her day. You've had your fun with this charade. I'll be back in character Sunday morning, but I'm taking tomorrow off."

The muscles in his jaw pulled tight and a coolness settled over his gaze. "You picked a fine time to turn coward on me."

"This isn't about fear, and it isn't about you."

"The hell it isn't."

She didn't see any use in continuing the conversation. Jesse had his mind made up and she could see he wasn't about to budge. "I'm sorry you feel that way."

The coolness in his eyes chilled her to the bone. It was the hard, unfriendly look he'd worn that first day in the tattoo shop.

It was tempting to cave in, to say she would go to the wedding stark naked if it would put a smile on his face. Anything to make what might be their last two days together happy ones.

Jesse shrugged off his jacket and headed for the closet.

Holly glanced at the bed. It was going to be a long night.

Jesse started to remove his shirt. Holly went into the bathroom to change.

I don't know what difference this makes. The guy's already seen you in nothing but your tattoos.

But for some reason she felt self-conscious about taking off her clothes in front of him.

When she returned to the bedroom, Jesse was in the sitting area with his laptop again.

"I'm going to bed now."

He didn't even look up. "Good night."

"'Night."

She climbed into bed, curling up on her side. The click of the computer keys was the only sound. In her mind she could visualize each click as a grain of sand

dropping through an hourglass, measuring out the
seconds and minutes that she had left with Jesse.

She wanted him to stop working, to come to bed
and make mad, passionate love to her all night long.

He did finally come to bed, but with the width of
the mattress, he seemed miles away. Holly waited for
some sign that he was in a receptive mood.

She was still waiting when she drifted off into a
restless sleep.

Jesse knew exactly when Holly fell asleep. Her
breathing changed and she seemed to settle deeper
into her pillow.

He missed the feel of her in his arms. Funny how
after only two nights of having her in bed with him,
he'd gotten that used to it.

She was being so stubborn about the question of
how she would dress at the wedding. She'd known up
front how he'd expected her to dress.

All week long she'd been walking around in provocative, sexy clothes, and had seemed perfectly
comfortable in them. The wedding was the grand fi-
nale of the week's events and he couldn't understand why all of a sudden Holly wanted to turn into
Mary Poppins.

She insisted she was doing it for Joanna, but he
couldn't see what it had to do with his sister. He was
still puzzling over the matter when he fell asleep.

Holly had been right.

Jesse realized it the moment he slipped into the

bedroom that was serving as bridal suite for the day and saw Joanna looking radiant in her wedding gown.

This was her day.

She smiled when she spotted him. "Hi, Jesse."

He worked his way through the bustle of brides-maids putting the finishing touches on their hair and makeup, and the photographer setting up his equipment, and stopped as close to Joanna as he could get without stepping on her dress. With both of them leaning from the waist, they managed a brief hug.

He took hold of her hand. "Well, this is it, kid."

"I know. Thank you so much for being here."

"What are big brothers for?"

"You're the best brother ever. I know how awkward it was for you to come here."

"At first," he admitted.

"You could have made it really unpleasant by copping an attitude or wearing a chip on your shoulder. But you've handled the whole situation like a real gentleman."

He wasn't about to contradict her, but he knew he wasn't the paragon she thought he was. He knew that his whole reason for bringing Holly had been part of a chip-wearing attitude. "I'm glad things have worked out."

"Do you know what I think? I think you've mellowed and I think Holly's behind it. She's the best thing that ever happened to you, Jesse."

A shaft of guilt slashed through him. He wished he'd told Joanna the truth about Holly from the beginning. His sister would be disappointed when she found out Holly wasn't going to be her sister-in-law after all.

But he'd have to cross that bridge when he came to it. Right now there was a wedding to attend.

He started toward the patio, where he was supposed to meet Douglas and the other ushers. As he strode past the open door of his father's office, Jesse Senior called to him. "Jesse, do you have a moment?"

He walked into the room. "Sure."

"Close the door, son."

This was the first time his father had called him son in years. He tried to hold on to the illusion that he didn't care, but there was a warm feeling in the pit of his stomach that told him otherwise. He closed the door.

"Your mother tells me that she invited you to the Christmas party this evening."

Ah, so that's what his father wanted, to tell him he wasn't welcome at the family event. Then why had he called him "son"? Old habit? "Yes, she did."

"I hope you're planning to attend. It would mean a great deal to your mother if you could be there."

Jesse was stunned by the revelation. "Holly and I will be at the Christmas party."

"Good." His father nodded. "I realize my next request is probably way out of line. And if I were in your position, my answer would be a flat-out no, but then, you never have reacted to things the same way I do. That's always been much of the problem between us. In this case, though, I'm sincerely hoping that you do have the opposite reaction than the one I would." He cleared his throat, then fell silent.

"What's the question?" Jesse prompted.

"Your mother would like to be included on the guest list for your wedding."

"My wedding?"

"Yes, when you and Holly get married."

Now wasn't the time to tell his father that he wasn't engaged—not when it was opening a door between him and his parents. A door that he wasn't sure had ever existed, even when he'd been a child.

He reached his hand forward to shake hands with his father. "Dad, you can tell Mother that when I get married, you'll both be invited."

Freestanding, stained-glass windows had been placed behind the altar. The lawn was neatly manicured and as smooth as a green carpet. Flowers were everywhere—red and white poinsettias and roses holding center stage.

Holly stood in line, waiting to be seated. Jesse had left their room before she'd dressed for the wedding, so she had no idea what his reaction to her attire would be.

She'd put on her makeup with a more subtle touch, constrained her hair in a French braid and wore an attractive, but conservative suit—a straight skirt of Christmas plaid reaching to several inches above her knee with a fitted jacket of emerald green. She was pleased with the results.

She hoped Jesse would be, too.

"Holly?" A feminine voice came from several feet behind her.

Holly turned and saw the last person she expected to see coming toward her. "Mother?"

Her mother reached Holly and briskly kissed the air by her cheeks. "Holly, dear."

Stepping out of the way, Diana Cutler beckoned her husband forward. He gave Holly the usual, cordial, stepfatherly hug.

"Howard, Mother, what a pleasant surprise."

Well, at least it was a surprise.

Diana looked quizzically at the people around Holly. "Are you here with friends, dear?"

"I'm here as a guest of one of the ushers."

Her mother quickly scanned the tuxedoed men seating the guests. "Well, I'm glad to see that you're finally socializing with people besides the biker crowd Red hangs out with."

"Actually, Mother, I met my date for the wedding at Dad's shop, and he does ride a motorcycle."

Her mother wrinkled her nose. "Holly, I hope you're teasing me."

Thinking of Jesse reminded her of the oversize rock on her left hand. With her hand at her side, she slowly turned the ring until the diamonds faced inward. That would really be the icing on the cake if her mother found out she was engaged.

There were only two days left in the engagement, but Holly had no doubt her mother would have her mother-of-the-bride dress bought and half the wedding planned in that short timespan.

Diana's gaze was wandering again. ''He's one of the ushers, you say?''

Holly knew her mother wouldn't let up until she'd been introduced.

Jesse was going to have to deal with more today than his fiancée's new image, he was going to have to meet his make-believe future in-laws.

Eleven

Jesse finally spotted Holly in the crowd waiting to be seated. It didn't surprise him that she'd gone through with her plans to dress conservatively. What knocked him right between the eyes was that while looking more sedate, she was nonetheless breathtaking.

He wondered if Holly realized that despite her efforts not to create a scene, she was likely to garner a share of attention anyway.

She was chatting with a man and woman standing next to her in line. When she spotted him, she smiled, but it was a tight, strained smile—not at all what he was used to from her. Was she afraid he was going to publicly make an issue about her clothes?

When he reached her, he started to give her a hug and kiss, the greeting having become second nature during the week of their mock engagement.

But Holly stepped back, placing her hand on his arm. "Jesse, guess who's here."

He looked more closely at the couple. They were an attractive pair, probably in their fifties. Neither one looked familiar. Whoever they were, they seemed to have the unflappable Holly rattled.

"Jesse, I'd like you to meet Diana and Howard Cutler. Mother, and Howard, Jesse Tyler."

Mother? This was Holly's mother and stepfather....

Running on automatic pilot, he got through the introductions and hand-shaking. Her parents didn't seem to know about the "engagement." Hopefully they wouldn't find out. He suspected that having to explain a broken engagement to her parents wouldn't be easy for Holly. Of course it might be easier than trying to explain why they would pretend to be engaged.

Diana was looked at him intently. He could almost feel the inevitable parental questions brewing in her mind: how long have they been dating, how serious is their relationship, are they sleeping together?

Before the conversation moved into those deeper waters, Holly said, "The rows are filling up. Maybe we should let Jesse seat us now."

Jesse seconded Holly's suggestion. He felt bad leaving her to deal with her parents alone, but he would rescue her after the wedding.

"He's adorable, hon. Take my advice and hang on to this one," Diana whispered to Holly once they were seated.

The last person she wanted advice about men from was her mother—the woman who wore Howard Cutler on her arm like some kind of trophy.

"He looks familiar. Have I met him before?"

She knew sooner or later her mother would realize who Jesse was, so she told her he was one of the owners of Yankee Motorworks.

"Oh. Definitely hang on to this one."

Luckily Holly was able to change the subject by asking about her stepsisters. She listened with half an ear as her mother talked on and on in muted tones until the wedding began.

Once the ceremony got under way, Holly tried to focus on what was going on. But her attention kept drifting to one particular usher who looked killer in his black tuxedo with red cummerbund and tie.

The man who had been her first lover.

The man she had fallen in love with.

Scary thought, but true. She was head-over-heels in love with Jesse Tyler.

During the exchanging of vows, a movement next to her caught her eye. Glancing to the side, she saw that Howard had reached over and taken her mother's hand. Turning, she caught a look pass between them. Like a lightning bolt it struck her that the two of them were in love.

She'd never noticed.

Because you were always too busy being bitter about the divorce.

To an eight-year-old wondering why her mother liked Howard better than her father, the money, which seemed the major difference between them, had appeared to be the logical answer. She hadn't considered it might be an emotional thing—that the two of them had fallen in love and had wanted to be together.

Her insistence on paying for her own education, her decision to avoid relationships with men until after she had a successful career, her whole future track had been plotted from premises sparked by bitterness. A bitterness, she now realized, that may have been founded on naive misconceptions.

Would it really matter if she married someone before she'd established her own career? For years she'd thought it would; she understood now that she'd been mistaken.

As long as she continued to work on her career goals after marriage rather than live off the glory of her husband's, it didn't matter what step of the process she was at before the wedding took place.

It seemed clear to her now, but she'd laid out her plan shortly after her parents' divorce and hadn't stopped to question it until today. The plan had been something solid for her to hold on to in those frightening days when her family, her whole world up to that point, had been crumbling around her.

So, where did that leave her now? And how did her feelings for Jesse fit into the new big picture?

The sounds of the recessional music burst into her muddled thoughts.

The wedding was over.

The reception was about to begin.

Between the wedding photos and the large numbers of people, it was a while before Jesse found Holly in the crowd. She had left her parents talking with another couple and was chatting with several of Jesse's relatives who had been horseback riding with her yesterday, when she felt his arm slip around her waist.

Smoothly, he maneuvered them away from the crowd and into the house until he found an empty room.

Once they were alone he said, "You look as though you've recovered from the shock of your parents' being here."

"Yes, I have. It was quite a surprise. Apparently Mother and Howard know Douglas's parents. Their beach condos are next door to each other."

"Did they notice your ring?"

"No, and hopefully they won't hear anything."

"Hopefully not. If they do, would you like to tell them the truth?"

She couldn't be sure her mother wouldn't make a scene. "It would probably be best just to let it go today. I could call and explain later."

"Whatever you think would be the best way to handle it. I hope there isn't any fallout from this to make things more awkward for you with your mother."

"Look, they might not hear anything. So there's really no need to worry about it yet."

"As an extra precaution, why don't you take off the ring?"

She slipped it off her finger. A surge of emotion washed through her. She almost slid the ring back into place. It was amazing how in such a short time it had come to feel so much a part of her. "Should I put it upstairs or would you like to hold on to it?"

He took it from her and slipped it into the inside pocket of his jacket. Holly felt an awkwardness she'd never felt around him before. She felt awkward, but also vulnerable.

Especially when he was looking at her the way he was.

Reaching out, he ran the tips of his fingers along the side of her neck. "You look beautiful today."

"Thank you." She longed to throw her arms around him and kiss him until he begged for mercy. To fight the urge, she reached out and tweaked his bow tie. "You're looking rather dapper yourself, sweetcheeks."

He started to say something, but instead leaned forward and kissed her. His lips were warm against hers, warm and incredibly wonderful.

"Oh, Jesse."

"Is something wrong?"

Only that I love you and tomorrow you'll be taking me home and I might never see you again except in magazines, on billboards or television.

But she couldn't say those words to him. "Don't you think we should be getting back to the wedding?"

"In a minute." He held her close, slowly running his hands over her back. "I want you to know that you were right about your outfit for today. And also about how out of line I was when I implied you might have seduced me to help you get the inside track on the designing job."

She wanted to hide behind a glib "I told you so," but she didn't. Instead she rested her head against his shoulder and tucked away all the memories of the moment—the feel of him holding her, the scent of his after-shave, the sounds of the reception in the distance, the afternoon sun glimmering on the polished hardwood floor.

Slowly she straightened, smoothed her hands down his lapels, and smiled. "Thank you."

"You're not going to gloat?"

"No." If they had to part, at least they could part on good terms. And if they had to part tomorrow, at least she would do her darnedest to enjoy the time they had left.

Holly did her best to stay upbeat, but as the day wore on she noticed Jesse seemed to be distancing himself from her. All week long when they'd been with a group, he'd kept her close by his side. Now he sometimes left her to mingle on her own, although she would occasionally look up to find him watching her. Watching her with a strange, unreadable expression on his face.

Jesse was puzzled. He'd spent the week with Holly and, if asked, would have said he knew her well. But watching her mingle made him wonder if he knew her at all. She blended right in with the wedding guests, it was difficult to imagine this was the same woman he'd first seen decked out in black leather.

He almost wished they had another week together so he could explore this other side of Holly.

Then again, there wasn't anything to prevent them from seeing each other in Daytona. But would she want to see him? Once the agreed-upon week was over, she might be perfectly happy and willing to have them go their separate ways.

He tried to convince himself that it didn't matter one way or another. Why should it? He could drop Holly off tomorrow, and have another woman on the back of his bike before the leather on the seat cooled.

But could any other woman take Holly's place?

She was unlike any other woman he'd ever known. And he couldn't imagine meeting anyone like her in the future. Holly was one of a kind.

Joanna had said Holly was the best thing that had happened to him. He'd sloughed it off at the time. Now he gave it serious consideration.

He couldn't remember the last time he'd felt so relaxed, so at ease. Well...most of the time. They'd had some disagreements, but overall their time together had been amiable.

Amiable wasn't the best label for their lovemaking—totally satisfying or mind-numbing were better, but still fell short.

So, what are you going to do about it...sweetcheeks?

At the luncheon in the grand ballroom, Holly sat at the head table with Jesse. The afternoon progressed with the traditional trimmings—the toasts, the cake cutting, the newlyweds' first dance and the gradual snowballing of couples starting with the parents and working through the bridal party.

When the open dancing began, Jesse returned to the table and claimed Holly.

The music was soft and dreamy. Combined with last night's restless sleep, the shock of seeing her mother today, and the warm male holding her, the music lulled her into a misty state. This was another moment she knew she would think about in the future.

Thinking over the week, she realized there were a lot of these special moments.

"Listen, Jess, in case I don't get the chance—" *or in case I chicken out...* "—I want to tell you I've enjoyed this week. And I'm glad we slept together, and that you were my first."

"Not just the first... Don't forget, the best," he teased, reminding her what she'd said to him the night they'd made love for the first time.

She smiled. "Yes, also the best."

"I've enjoyed this week, too, Holly."

Don't stop there! Tell me we'll see each other again. Ask me what my plans for next weekend are.

But Jesse remained silent.

The bride and groom left for their honeymoon with a fanfare and a shower of rice. Gradually the wedding guests began to leave until all that remained were the family members who had been invited to the Christmas party.

Sometime during the past half hour, probably when she'd been saying goodbye to her mother and stepfather, Holly lost track of Jesse. He wasn't in their room when she checked, and a quick glance around the living room didn't produce results, either.

The Christmas tree was lit. Carols were playing, accompanying the happy sounds of children. There were a dozen or so little ones, but it was hard to tell for sure because they were outnumbered by grown-ups and didn't stay long enough in one spot for an accurate head count. Waiters roamed through the crowd with an assortment of hors d'oeuvres and drinks.

Holly mingled, hoping to spot Jesse in the process. She was talking—or rather, listening—to one of Jesse's cousins from Texas when a small, high-pitched voice announced, "Santa's coming!"

"Santa! Santa!" Other young voices joined the chant.

There was the sound of the front door slamming and a wild ringing of jingle bells. The adults guided the children to the Christmas tree as the jingling came closer. A deep, booming, "Ho, ho, ho," announced Santa's arrival into the living room.

Holly was busy watching the children's reactions and didn't look at the new arrival himself until he passed at close range.

Santa wore the traditional suit of red velvet and white fur. He had a wide black belt wrapped around a padded waistline. White whiskers and white hair gave the impression of great age.

When Holly looked at Santa's face, a pair of familiar green eyes met hers. If that wasn't enough, Santa's sexy smile was a dead giveaway.

Jesse.

He took his position in front of the tree, first passing out the presents underneath, then opening the overstuffed burlap bag he'd carried in with him.

A flurry of paper and ribbons managed to stay one step ahead of the uniformed servants gathering the debris and spiriting it away in plastic bags.

Santa reached deep into his pack. "One last present," he announced.

"For me?" asked a small fellow, holding a shiny new fire engine and sucking on a candy cane.

Jesse looked at her. "No, this one's for Holly."

"Can I deliver it?"

Jesse handed the package to him. "Sure, sport." He pointed Holly out to his pint-size helper.

Holly accepted the package. "Thank you."

"You're welcome," the child said, then took off, wailing like the siren of a fire engine.

Holly looked at the present. The box was about the size of a coffee mug. The tag read To Holly, From Santa.

Her gaze flew to Jesse. He had moved closer, and was now only a few steps away. Taking her by the hand, he led her to a quiet corner.

At his urging, she slowly removed the red velvet ribbon and gold foil wrapping, then opened the box. Peeling back the tissue paper revealed a leather ring box.

She opened it and glanced down. "The holly ring! How did you get this?"

Jesse chuckled. "I bought it."

"But we saw it in Daytona several weeks ago."

"I went Christmas shopping yesterday. The jeweler has another shop at the mall here. They called Daytona and had the ring sent down. Do you like it?"

"That's a silly question. Of course I love it, but..." How to phrase this without seeming over-anxious, pushy or desperate? She wanted so urgently for it to mean what she thought it might, but she was afraid to hope. "It's a bit extravagant for a Christmas present."

"I meant the ring to be a Christmas present when I bought it."

Her hopes plummeted. "Well, as I remember the day we were ring shopping, you mentioned I could save it until I met the man I was really going to marry. But—"

"If I remember correctly, your answer at the time was that the only man you would marry would be Santa Claus."

"Yes."

"So will you?" He reached into the box and removed the ring, then locked her gaze with his. "Will you marry Santa?"

She raised her hand to stop her bottom lip from quivering and blinked quickly to hold off any tears. "Yes." Her voice was shaky, but Jesse must have understood because he slipped the ring on her finger, then pulled her into his arms for a hug.

"I love you, Holly."

"I love you, too."

"Even if I don't cry over *Old Yeller?*"

"Yes." She hugged him again. "You've put on a few pounds since we danced at the wedding," she said, patting his padded stomach.

"You don't like my new image? And here I thought I was turning myself into the man of your dreams."

"You already were the man of my dreams."

"So I can lose the padding and you'll still have me?"

"Lose the padding, the beard, the suit...whatever."

"There are some of those whatevers I'd like to discuss in more detail later. But first I need to get my reindeer off the roof."

Epilogue

Christmas Day

Holly put the last few stitches in the hem of her white lace skirt. "Done."

Ellen cheered. "Nothing like just in the nick of time."

"Give me a break. I only had two weeks." And she'd made the maid- and matron-of-honor dresses for Ellen and Joanna first. She slipped into the skirt and fastened it. "Besides, it's still an hour before the wedding."

Joanna was on the other side of the hotel room where the women were getting ready for the ceremony, looking out the window to the street ten floors below. "The road out front is packed with media vans and photographers," she said.

There was a knock at the door.

"If that's my father, he's early," Holly said.

"And if it's not?" Ellen asked, heading for the door.

"It had better not be my brother," Joanna said. "He can't see Holly until the wedding."

"And if it's a reporter, tell him 'no comment.'" Holly had been badgered by the media since the day she and Jesse had applied for a marriage license.

The last Yankee Hunk wedding was indeed big news.

Holly heard Ellen gasp and quickly turned around. Standing in the doorway was the second most gorgeous specimen of manhood she'd ever seen—Jesse would always be first, of course.

"Another one of the Yankee Hunks, I presume," Holly said.

The dark-haired man stepped into the room, followed by an equally appealing blonde. "Both of the other Yankee Hunks, actually."

"And the women who love them." A smiling brunette swept into the room, passed the two men and hugged Holly. "I'm Genie, and I'm so happy for you."

"I recognize your voice from the phone call about the baby."

"Speaking of the baby, this is Callie," Genie introduced her to a blonde who was standing hand-in-hand with the dark-haired man.

"If you're Callie. You must be Rorke," Holly said. "Where's the little guy?"

"Michael Harrison O'Neil is home in Vermont being spoiled by his two grandpas," Rorke said.

"After you and Jesse get home from your honeymoon, have him bring you to Harrison for a visit," Callie offered.

Holly turned to the blond man. "You must be Alex, then."

"I am. I also want some of your time when you get back. We have a clothing line to discuss, and I want a new uniform for next year's racing team."

"You liked the sketches?"

"I liked the sketches."

Holly introduced the newcomers to Ellen and Joanna. They talked until there was another knock on the door.

This time it was her father and the wedding photographer. Rorke, Callie, Alex and Genie set off in search of Jesse.

"I was beginning to think I was going to have to be my own best man," Jesse said when Rorke and Alex joined him outside the hotel ballroom, where in a short time he and Holly would be married.

"We stopped to see the bride," Rorke said.

"You've seen Holly?"

"Yes," Alex said. "You didn't think we would let you marry someone without us checking her out first? What kind of friends would we be if we did that?"

"So, what's the verdict?" Jesse asked.

Alex gave him a thumbs up, then moved out of the way so Callie and Genie could give Jesse a hug and extend their congratulations.

The florist came up to the men with their boutonnieres. The woman was pinning Jesse's on when Rorke asked, "I know it's Christmas and all, Jesse, but do you really want a miniature Santa climbing a rosebud?"

"It's a long story."

Rorke and Alex exchanged glances. "I'll bet Holly knows," Rorke said.

"You're probably right," Alex agreed.

They continued talking until the guests began to arrive. Rorke and Alex began seating the arrivals, and Jesse stepped over to have a few words with Chad Ralston.

"I've known since October that this day was coming," Chad said. "I felt it in the air when we were in the tattoo shop."

"You'd probably had too much sun."

Chad shook his head. "No, the way you two were looking at each other was a dead giveaway."

Jesse chuckled. "If you say so." Over Chad's shoulder, he spotted his parents and his brother-in-law. Although his father had asked that they be invited, Jesse hadn't been sure they would actually show up—but here they were.

He excused himself from Chad and went over to the florist to collect his mother's corsage and his father's boutonniere. The flowers served as an icebreaker, getting them through the first awkward moments.

"I never expected to be both mother-of-the-bride and mother-of-the-groom in the same month," Mimi Tyler said.

"It's interesting how things worked out," Jesse Senior said.

"Yes, it is," Jesse agreed.

The ballroom was decorated for the Christmas holiday, but the view out the windows behind the minister was Florida sunshine and the turquoise surf of the Atlantic Ocean. It was a beautiful sight, but it didn't hold Holly's interest long.

Once the music began, and she started into the room on her father's arm, the only thing she focused on was the man waiting for her.

The last two weeks had been so hectic, she and Jesse hadn't gotten to spend nearly as much time together as she'd wanted to. But that would change soon.

At the end of the aisle, Red gave his daughter a hug. "Be happy, Holly," he whispered.

"I will, Dad."

Together they turned, and Red held her hand out toward her groom. Jesse stepped forward and locked hands with her.

She listened to the words of the service, but she found herself compelled again and again to look at the man standing by her side.

This was it!

Soon she would be Jesse's wife. For better or worse and everything in between.

After they shared their first kiss as man and wife, her gaze lowered and she caught a glimpse of his boutonniere. She did a double take, then bit her bottom lip to keep from laughing.

"I like your Santa."

Jesse smiled.

"I told you Holly would know," Rorke said to Alex.

The newlyweds walked down the aisle together, past the small, select group of family and friends. Holly had been surprised, but pleased, when Jesse had told her that his parents had wanted to be invited.

The photographer took over, arranging everyone for pictures. At Jesse's request he included a Yankee group photo—Jesse and Holly, with Rorke and Callie, and Alex and Genie.

"I can see that on a magazine cover," Ellen told Holly.

"I want an autographed copy to hang in the tattoo shop," Red said.

"Tattoo shop?" Rorke asked.

"Yes, my dad's a tattoo artist."

Alex smiled. "You wouldn't know anything about a Yankee Go Home tattoo, would you?"

"Actually, I do."

Rorke and Alex exchanged glances. "We should have known," Alex said.

"This certainly explains why he was making such a big deal over it," Rorke said.

"That's enough, guys," Jesse said. "Come on, let's celebrate."

The group was small, but they were lively. There was the continual murmur of conversation and plenty of laughter throughout the afternoon.

When it was time for the toast, Rorke and Alex stood.

Rorke raised his champagne glass. "Since I've been married the longest, I'm going to pull seniority here and go first. As you know, Alex, Jesse and I have been blessed. First with our friendship and second with the success of our business. The media said we had it all, but each of us was missing one thing. Love. We were missing love. Then Callie came back into my life and Alex found Genie. Now that Jesse has Holly in his life, we truly have it all. Here's to the future."

"There's not much I can add," Alex said. "But Genie and I wish Jesse and Holly as much happiness as we've found. I'd also like to toast the other new member of the Yankee family, Michael O'Neil. And all the other O'Neils, Daltons and Tylers to come."

Red, Jesse Senior, and Howard Cutler also offered toasts to the newlyweds.

During the toasts the band had arrived. When they began to play, Jesse claimed his bride. "I believe this first dance is mine, Mrs. Tyler."

Once he had her in his arms on the dance floor, she whispered in his ear, "You'll always be my first, Jesse."

"And the best?"

"Always the best."

*   *   *   *   *

SILHOUETTE® *Desire®*

COMING NEXT MONTH

MILLION DOLLAR SWEEPSTAKES (III)

 **Are your lips
succulent, impetuous,
delicious or racy?**

Find out in a very special Valentine's Day
promotion—THAT SPECIAL KISS!

Inside four special Harlequin and Silhouette February
books are details for THAT SPECIAL KISS!
explaining how you can have your lip prints read
by a romance expert.

Look for details in the following series books,
written by four of Harlequin and Silhouette readers'
favorite authors:

Silhouette Intimate Moments #691
Mackenzie's Pleasure by *New York Times*
bestselling author Linda Howard

Harlequin Romance #3395
Because of the Baby by Debbie Macomber

Silhouette Desire #979
Megan's Marriage by Annette Broadrick

Harlequin Presents #1793
The One and Only by Carole Mortimer

Fun, romance, four top-selling authors, plus a **FREE**
gift! This is a very special Valentine's Day you won't
want to miss! Only from Harlequin and Silhouette.

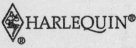

You're About to Become a *Privileged Woman*

Reap the rewards of fabulous free gifts and benefits with proofs-of-purchase from Silhouette and Harlequin books

Pages & Privileges™

It's our way of thanking you for buying our books at your favorite retail stores.

PROOF OF PURCHASE
SD-PP83
Offer expires October 31,1996

Pages & Privileges ™

**Harlequin and Silhouette—
the most privileged readers in the world!**

For more information about Harlequin and Silhouette's PAGES & PRIVILEGES program call the Pages & Privileges Benefits Desk: 1-503-794-2499

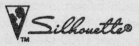

Silhouette®

SD-PP83